Broken Family Ties

a novel
by
PC Marks

A PC Marks Publication
http://stores.lulu.com/phyl4ya

Copyright © by PC Marks

PC Marks Publication

PO Box 18429

Cleveland OH 44118

Visit www.pcpcmarks.com

ISBN 978-0-6151-6093-1

Library of Congress control number 2007906929

Dedicated to my family, Malcolm Jr., Phylicia, and Jeresa

& Jerell.

Broken Family Ties

By

PC Marks

Chapter 1

Changing Faces

Kevin and Ann Lee Grover were in the midst of raising their three children. Caroline is the middle child and only girl.

Caroline Grover is a tall thin child. Her skin is a beautiful caramel color complimented by bright brown eyes. All of the adult ladies would kill for her silky tar black hair.

Looking at such a beautiful child, intelligent beyond her years, some would say she is destined for greatness.

Caroline and her brothers Carl and Charles didn't have to leave their home. The Grandparents Henry and Alicia Brooks eagerly took over the massive house.

The Grover children's grandmother Alicia Brooks aged well. A hint of how pretty she was as a youth shows through her smooth tan skin. Her natural salt and pepper hair is worn in a neat bun at the nape of her neck. Her piercing black eyes betray her innermost thoughts. Agile for an older woman, she moves with the grace of a gazelle. Her tongue is equally as swift.

She treated everyone as though they were beneath her. Alicia felt people should strive to get to her level. She saw herself as superior to the common folk of her surroundings.

Alicia loved God and her family. She was cordial to her neighbors but never too friendly. For all the years she lived in the neighborhood she never invited them in to her home.

Alicia's daily routine was working the land, cleaning the house and praising the Lord.

She was called by her first name in church once. Her reply was "I am Mrs. Brooks, I don't recall formally being introduced by my first name," her lips curled up, those cold black eyes challenging. "Are you part of my family? Those are the only people who I allow to call me Alicia. I shall be called Mrs. Brooks unless you are of blood relation?"

The member stared in disbelief at such unchristian like behavior. Alicia's menacing smile didn't fade as she watched the fidgeting member fumbling over her apologetic words.

Alicia felt she was deserving of the ill begotten home of her less than God like daughter.

Chapter 2

Saving Graces

Henry Brooks was the best substitute father and a Godsend to any child. He was a grayish-brown man with a huge lanky frame reminiscent of a younger athlete. His receding hair line had soft gray hairs half circling his huge head. There in his dark eyes lived a man who had been through some things.

Henry was happy to step in as guardian for his three beautiful grandchildren. He wasn't thrilled with the circumstances of how it came to be. He accepted the devastating blow as God's will.

Henry never knew his father. His mother was very stern. She reared fourteen children, six boys and eight girls. Henry being the oldest of the boys was the bread winner. He sent money home regularly but never returned. Not even for his mother's funeral.

Carl, the oldest of the Grover children is two years Caroline's senior. He was a tall child. His milk chocolate skin matched his dreamy brown eyes. His parent's kept his curly black hair cropped close to his head. Carl's large hands and feet looked out of place on his rail thin frame.

He was like a sponge, soaking in his surroundings, always questioning. And very protective of those he loved.

Carl remembered both his parents well. His fondest memories were of his mother Ann.

Ann was a tall woman. Her daughter had inherited her caramel complexion. She was slim; her hourglass figure didn't allow her to fit into the skinny class. Her beautiful brown eyes shined brightly. Ann usually stood out in a crowd. She had high cheek bones, long limbs. Her graceful, confident walk turned heads. Her long flowing soft black hair was always perfect, never a string out of place.

Ann didn't have many friends. On occasion, neighbors and church members would stop by. She would become flustered and tongue tied, unable to hold an adult conversation. Her comfort zone was with her family.

Chapter 3

Parents Again

Caroline had her mother's attention before nap time.

While she napped, Carl and his mother watched cartoons.

Quietly sitting on the couch Ann began to feel nauseated.

"Carl, bring me a ginger ale," she asked.

Carl returned to see his mother vomiting into the

trash can by the side of her chair. He dropped the ginger

ale. He ran outside to find his Dad.

"Daddy, daddy, Mommy's throwing up!" He yelled

tugging at his father's shirt tail.

Kevin rushed in to the house. "Ann, are you okay?"

he asked. He stood there watching her. She stared at her

husband. His captivating brown eyes stared into hers. He was of average height. His body type was what the average man paid to obtain at the gym.

The room lit up. He returned an illuminating smile.

Carl asked, "What? Why are you both smiling? Mommy's sick." His question was interrupted by Caroline's awakening cry.

The three walked upstairs to her nursery. The parents couldn't stop smiling. The smiling turned into laughter.

"You're going to have a new sister or brother," Ann announced. Kevin picked up his son swinging and dancing around the nursery.

The baby was born six months later weighing a little over five pounds. A beautiful baby boy was presented to his parents. His caramel colored skin was inherited from his mother and sister. His eyes were reminiscent of his older brother in shape only. He did not have the height of his siblings. The parents lovingly teased that his height would be inherited from Kevin's side of the family.

Kevin was pleased to meet his new son Charles. Standing their holding the new addition, he relived his reaction to their first son, Carl. Kevin was always in awe of his first born. He didn't want to harm him in anyway. He was scared of him and later would admit a little jealous of the attention his beloved Ann showered on Carl.

Chapter 4

Male Bonding

Kevin was a self employed truck driver. He had landed contracts in Michigan and New York.

Carl asked his dad why he was rarely home. He was curious about the payment arrangements with some of the locals. He had overheard his mother complaining to his dad. "We are going to go broke if you don't start charging everyone full price," Ann said.

Kevin's response was "If you forget where you come from you can't figure where you're going. If it wasn't for someone giving me a break, there's no telling where I would be today. With all the blessings bestowed upon me, God would never forgive me if I didn't help my

brothers and sisters where I could."

Carl never viewed his father as a Good Samaritan

let alone a Christian man. Kevin attended church regularly.

He was usually spotted in the parking lot shooting the

breeze, running into the sanctuary minutes before the

service started every Sunday.

Carl asked if he could go on a delivery route.

Kevin agreed.

"I figure you getting 'bout tall enough to drive.

You need to put on some weight to haul merchandise. It's

got to be packed just right, delivered on time and in good

shape. Hell you can't even lift what I consider the small

boxes," Kevin chuckled. "When I get up in age my boys

will be taking over the family business," he continued

proudly. "Don't you ever regret it either because you asked

for it," Kevin said.

Carl was thrilled. He and his dad became fast buddies. On occasion they scheduled weekend trips traveling from Cleveland Ohio to Detroit Michigan. They discussed Carl's future, his responsibility as the leader of the family if anything should happen to Kevin.

Chapter 5

A Troubled Soul

Charles was a little stubby butter ball. The hand me downs of his older brother all had to be shortened in length, let out in width. The caramel skin color of his mother had begun to darken. The almond colored eyes of his brother remained.

Sunday's were family day for the five of them. The family got dressed for church. They stayed for the dinner. After church the family day would continue at home.

Carl rarely remembered his father participating. His brother was too young but seemed to be enjoying himself. He would dance or gurgle something unintelligible. The whole family would be full of coos and awes. The giggling fest would ensue and all was happy with the Grover family until Caroline would end it.

Caroline always smiled as a baby, never fussy. Still she was disconnected. Ann had taken her in for testing at six months old.

Caroline would sit in her crib for hours staring at the ceiling and smiling. Ann would drop things, come in singing making all sorts of noises. Caroline wouldn't budge. Ann would turn on the radio, no response. She would turn up the TV, no response. She decided it was time to find out what was going on with her daughter.

Kevin and Ann dressed the baby and strapped her into the family station wagon headed to the Cleveland Clinic Ear, Nose and Throat specialist.

It was a quiet ride. Neither party wanted to discuss the what-ifs. They arrive at the clinic, check in at the front desk and take a seat in the waiting room. Patiently they

wait to be called.

Kevin looks around the waiting room. Some of the

toddler age children are shy and clinging to their parents.

Others are playing with children they just met today. All

have a glow of innocence in their eyes. He pulls the

blanket off of his six month old daughter. She's staring at

the ceiling, her tiny lips eerily curved.

His first thought is of Ann's mother Alicia.

She tried to convince Ann and Kevin to abort.

Ann's mother was going on about a family curse

and the seventh female child born. It was as though Alicia

was having an outer body experience. She was speaking

out loud. "The seventh girl child in the family should not

live! Grandma Emma was touched by the devil. The child

will be the devil reincarnated. We have to pray, pray for

forgiveness, get rid of it, and pray for forgiveness!"

Kevin snatched his son and wife running the hell out of the Brooks household promising to never return.

Ann bargained with God while they waited to be called. *God you gave me a great Dad, a great husband and the beginnings of two great children. I know you had your reasons for Caroline. I live my life by your rules. I even honor thy mother despite all the things that happened. Please God, don't let my baby be my mother's seventh child. I will continue to serve to the best of my ability. I know I fall short at times but Lord you know I'm trying. I need to ask rather it be thy will that my child is normal and happy.* Ann turns to Kevin.

"It happened six months ago and I told you I don't ever want the subject brought up again. You deal with your mother." Kevin exited the waiting room abruptly in need of a smoke.

Upon his return, the Grover baby was called. Ann studies

the expression on the doctor's face. She can't quite

determine if it is going to be good news.

"Mr. and Mrs. Grover are you God fearing citizens

of the state of Ohio," the doctor begins.

Both parents look at each other and back to the

doctor.

"There is nothing medically wrong with your

daughter. Her hearing is fine. I asked the question because

I am also an ordained minister," he paused. "I've been

trained to know when the devil is stewing. I don't want to

alarm you about your daughter's medical health. At this

time I am talking to you as a minister. That baby's soul is

in trouble," he says pointing at Caroline.

Ann froze, her mouth open, staring. She took a deep

breath before speaking. "Dr. Holland I don't quite follow,"

she said, one eyebrow raised. "I brought my baby in here

for a hearing test. I don't see how her immortal soul has

come into play within the ten minutes you spent looking

into her ears. Are you trying to tell me you could see her

soul through her ear? That doesn't make any sense." Her

hand on her hip head cocked to one side, she continued,

"My husband and I are God fearing Christians. Just like

you and your family we attend church regularly. We

practice the word and share it with our children. Caroline

will be brought up in the church with our same beliefs," she

said.

Ann turned to Kevin. Kevin turned away. He

located the door and made a quick exit. "I'll be back. I need

a smoke," he said.

"Just because you're a man of the cloth does not

mean you were truly called by God. I am not judging just

stating facts. Where do you get off calling my daughter the

devil," Ann continued.

The Reverend Dr. Holland listened intently. This was not the first time he was faced with something similar to the Grover baby. He had seen this earlier in his practice.

As an ordained minister Dr. Holland was ready to battle the devil for Christ. His first love was being a doctor before he was called to the ministry about thirty years ago.

Dr Holland excused himself, apologized for offending the Grover family, reassured Ann that he was trying to help and gave his office phone number to the hospital as well as his personal line at church.

Before walking away, he tried to reach Ann one last time. "Mrs. Grover, I am here for you if you need to talk or have questions concerning Caroline's medical… or mental health."

He returned to his office. His assistant cancelled all of his appointments for the day. When asked why, Doctor

Holland replied, "I need to talk to God about this thing

happening twice in my life."

Chapter 6

The Baby Girl

Ann never filled Kevin in on the talk she had with the quack Reverend Dr. Holland as she sarcastically called him. He never asked and she didn't volunteer to relay the dreadful diagnosis on her second born child's soul.

Ann took Caroline to an Ear Nose and Throat specialist at University Hospitals for a second opinion. She changed the children's pediatrician citing to her husband "The man is crazy."

There was something different in Caroline's eyes. Ann refused to believe in the demon seed nonsense Dr. Quack and her mother were spewing.

Though Caroline was a beautiful child there was something disconcerting about her. It made her ugly inside. She thrived on creating tension and awkward situations.

Caroline stared at her siblings, a cold hard look. She smiled at inappropriate times. Everyone noticed this about Caroline. Ann just couldn't bring herself to discuss it aloud. She would talk to God.

Caroline had ruined a family day gathering. She was jumping up and down, her bangs flying in the air. Her two long pigtails were threatening to come undone. She was pretty in her pink satin Sunday dress with matching shoes, gloves and purse-unable to contain herself screaming, "me next, me next".

"Okay miss ants in the pants, what you got to say," Ann asked smiling brightly.

Kevin stayed but the impression on his face was less than enthusiastic.

Caroline chimed in with her little squeaky five year old voice, "I saw you kiss that man at church and it wasn't Daddy." Her head was turning from side to side, lips pursed. "You hugged and kissed him like it were daddy but it wasn't," she teased. "You going to hell aren't you?"

Before Ann would be given a chance to answer, Caroline was still taunting her parents. Her little white teeth displayed. She was talking to her mother, staring at her father. Kevin's facial expression was stoic.

Caroline had her mother's beautiful smile but on her face it was cynical, evil really.

"Daddy's gone leave us because you nasty. He will spend an eternity in burning fires with you for leaving us. I learned that in the big people Sunday school earlier today. I sat in the back in your class mommy. Your class was talking about a word I can't remember. The teacher

said it meant you were breaking one of those comments.

I'm a big girl huh?"

Caroline laughing hysterically abruptly stopped.

She stared eye to eye at her mother, the evil smile

darkening her pretty bright face.

The family was stunned into quietness. Kevin

immediately left the front room. He replayed that visit to

Dr. Holland over and over in his head. The words were

engraved vividly in his mind. "That child's soul is in

trouble." He had stood around the corner listening.

Kevin decided tonight would be the night he would

quit running and face the problem head on with his wife.

He decided that he would tell Ann of things he saw and

heard Caroline do. First, he decided to look up Dr.

Holland. He was glad that he picked up the business card

Ann had discarded.

Kevin went out back to smoke. At times he joked they were given the wrong baby at the hospital. He knew it wasn't true. It made it easier to deal with at times. A lot easier than believing in Alicia's seventh child crap.

Kevin would never say it aloud, just always told Ann from the time Caroline was born, "We're going to have our hands full with this one." He had spent countless nights praying for his child and his mother-n-law's soul.

"Caroline, that isn't true. You're telling a story dear. I have encouraged you to use your imagination for good things. One day, you'll be a great story teller. As you grow into adulthood, you'll be a vibrant writer as long as you are able to distinguish truth from lies. Haven't we discussed this time and time again? "If you make up hurtful stories its not funny, do you understand," Ann explained.

She continued. "For you to tell your father that I dare kiss another man at church is inappropriate. It's incredulous. I think you hurt him. You need to tell him that you make up stories all the time and went too far this time. What do you think?"

Caroline continued staring at her mother. An unnerving curl of her lips across her face. She would not speak. She nodded her head toward her mother.

"The word your looking for that you can't pronounce is adultery." Ann continued. "It is the seventh commandment and says *Thou shall not commit adultery.*" Ann spelled it out for her and then sounded it out, *a-d-u-l-t-e-r-y,* adultery." She watched her daughter before continuing.

"You're about to get a lesson in the ninth commandment. It says *Thou shall not bear false witness against thine neighbor.* Caroline this commandment means that you should not tell lies. Again, it's okay to tell a made up story for fun. When a story that you know is not true is told to hurt someone, it is called sin. Do you understand? You have done this several times. I will pray for you and ask that you do the same for me. I am not going to punish you because I believe you are confused."

Ann continued to talk. "I love you Caroline and I believe you love me. Please explain to me why you continue to act in this manner?"

Ann's list of excuses for her child was the length of her arm. The ones she used most often, "She just has a mean streak. She's beautiful and spirited. I was like that myself growing up. I used to drive momma crazy with my wild tales. I turned out alright. There is nothing wrong with my child." Ann repeated several times to the family, church members or whom ever else Caroline attacked.

The boys were told to go with their father outside in the backyard. Ann was determined not to let this cute little carbon copy of her when the war tonight.

Caroline was inappropriately smiling. "Mommy, you are a liar. You said that we shouldn't tell lies but stories are okay as long as we know they're make-believe. I told a true story and now you're trying to get me to lie. I love you mommy but I can't go to hell with you."

It was time to face the music. Something wasn't quite right with her daughter.

"Caroline, everybody kisses on Sunday morning or shake hands or show some sort of affection to God's people when we're gathered together. It is called fellowship. If I kissed a man in church, it's okay as long as I didn't kiss him like I kiss your dad."

Although smiling, Caroline's eyes showed pure hatred. She continued taunting her mother. "I understand you don't want daddy to know," she countered with a roll of her eyes. "I think if you weren't doing anything wrong, you wouldn't care if he knew."

Ann placed her hands to her temples and began to massage. She didn't want to send her daughter away thinking she was mad. She refused to resort to her mother's tactics of beating the crap out of a confused child. She tried reasoning with her daughter one last time.

"Caroline, your daddy knows the man I kissed at church. He's a deacon and one of your daddy's friends. Your dad left the room because of your story so he has already heard it. It's the proper thing to do in church. You're too young for me to explain adultery. If you weren't such a busy body and had attended your Sunday school class you would not be confused. This would be a good time for you to go to your room and think about your actions," Ann stated in a firm but even toned voice.

Chapter 7

Family Secrets

Ann tucked Caroline in. She went into the nursery to check on Charles who was fast asleep then went out back looking for Kevin and Carl. She knew he would be tinkering with the old Chevy truck his deceased dad left him. As Ann walked up to the truck she was concerned.

"What's wrong little man, she asked of her first born.

Before Carl could respond Kevin intervened. "Hey, love of my life. What are you doing out here in the male quarters," he asked smiling.

Ann rushed to Carl's side. She started wiping his tears away.

Kevin gently removed her hands from their son's face. "The boy just upset with your daughter. I'm explaining some church stuff to him. I think I got him a little shaky. What you come out here for any way girl?"

Kevin always referred to her as girl, even though she had three kids, she felt like a girl in his presence.

"A girl can't approach her man without wanting something, I just wanted to know where my other two favorite men were. I see I am intruding on some serious man talk. You can find me when you boys are done fixing this raggedy car," she said walking away giggling like a school girl.

Before returning to the house, she winked at her first born. Carl smiled. She looked around outside admiring her land and house. Her eyes landed on Caroline's window.

Ann thought Kevin is right, Dr Quack is right. Momma may have been right but I could not have aborted my child.

Caroline was wearing one of her mother's night gowns and prancing in front of the window deliberately defying her mother. Caroline was the spitting image of Ann's mother Alicia.

She remembered the agreement with Kevin to never mention the incident of Alicia's ranting. Ann wanted to talk to some one desperately about the things her mother said. Kevin was her best friend. He wouldn't discuss it. The neighbors were not trustworthy. She knew too many stories of one neighbor befriending another to be ridiculed and betrayed.

Ann had told Caroline time and time again to stop going through her things. She chose a few tattered items to give to Caroline. Caroline would refuse to wear them.

She said to her mother "I only like wearing pretty things so daddy loves me like you."

Chapter 8

New York Bound

Kevin and Ann always took a weekend trip to New York every year. Business is booming Ann has a part time job at the school. She's off all summer which she loves. It gives her time with the children. Everything is going just fine.

The first two children were older. They were becoming less dependent. Carl is seven, Caroline, five. Carl is protective of Charles, he's two.

Normally they would stay a weekend. Kevin had convinced Ann to stay an entire week. They can't remember the last time it was just the two of them for a whole week.

Ann arranged for her parents to baby sit. She didn't mention to Kevin or her dad, she had to pay Momma Alicia and promised that she could stay at their house.

Her mother flatly told her, "Your kids are not welcomed in my house. They don't know the Lord. That daughter would leave evil spirits behind. I'd be throwing holy water for a year if I let her in my front door."

Ann didn't want to disappoint Kevin. All he could talk about for a month was this one week trip to New York. He had some big surprise in store for Ann but would only give hints.

The clothes were packed. The house was sparkling clean to live up to Grandma Alicia standards. The children were fed, dressed appropriately and sent outside.

Caroline was to read *Three Little Pigs* to her brothers. This assured Ann that the boys wouldn't get dirty before Grandma Alicia's arrival.

Ann's mother treated her more like a trophy to be treasured in the presence of others. She ignored her when they were alone. It made Ann sad that she was having the kids get dressed up as if they were little show ponies. She thought to herself, they should be out playing and getting dirty. She quickly put those thoughts of her childhood out of her mind and reminded herself how lucky she was. Half the neighbor's husbands went out of town on a regular basis. They never considered asking their wives to tag along.

It kind of made her smile to think of the envy all the other housewives must feel. She recanted those thoughts with prayer. *God forgive me for being vain and thank you for blessing me with Kevin.*

The children went to the picnic table behind the
house, all dolled up. Caroline announced disdain in how
they were being treated.

"How dare Ann have us sit out in this hot ass sun
dressed like we are headed for church just because
Grandma Alicia is coming!"

Carl responded. "You know Grandma Alicia hate
for us to come in her house because she thinks we're not
saved. Mommy is just trying to keep some peace in the
family Caroline. You know she gone start spraying that
holy water all over the house as soon as mommy and daddy
leaves," he laughed.

Charles giggled and tugged at his brother, pointing,
"book."

Caroline went storming off toward the garage.
Charles followed. Carl sat there on the bench as the
obedient son he aimed to be.

Grandpa Henry and Grandma Alicia arrived just before dark as planned. Caroline was pretty in pink. She had changed into her pink sundress, white lace socks with white shoes, a pink and white satin ribbon holding her shoulder length hair in a messy pony tail.

Charles was dressed in his khaki colored slacks, short sleeved white oxford shirt with his brown church shoes.

Carl was dressed in his black slacks, white golf shirt and black shoes Ann had originally dressed him in.

The kids were the picture of health, happiness and cleanliness it appeared. Ann took a second look back at the three of them. A broad smile on her face looking at the younger two, "We'll discuss the outfit changes later. Good choices though," she said. "Carl you're always the perfect little boy." Off she went to greet her Dad. She was always so happy to see him.

For a moment she thought maybe this trip to New York was just what Kevin needed. She would try to convince him to become closer to Caroline. The distance between the two was obvious. She could only imagine what everyone else thought.

"Hi Daddy," Ann was at the truck before Grandpa Henry could put it in park. Kevin was walking slowly behind her. He liked to watch the interaction from a distance. He often wondered if he and Caroline would ever become so close.

Ann was kissing and hugging her dad as if she hadn't seen him in months. The two had dinner less than a week ago.

Henry was beaming. He was just as happy to see Ann. Alicia's reaction to the father daughter reunion was no surprise.

"Well hello Ann, your daddy is not the only person doing you this huge favor of watching the spawn of the

devil. You would think the least I would get is a hello,"
Alicia said in a dry, I could be doing something better with
my time tone.

. "Mother, I didn't mean to ignore you. I know
Daddy wasn't feeling well so it was great to see him
looking good and a blessing from above that you don't
have to baby sit my children alone. I am thrilled to see the
both of you," Ann said.

Ann was smiling in her father's direction. Henry
was smiling back. He refused to allow Alicia to ruin his
fun with his only child and his beautiful grandchildren.

The children were kissed assured they were loved.
Kevin and Ann filled with excitement were on their way to
New York, New York the big Apple.

Chapter 9

Grandparent's Rules

Alicia was awakened in the wee hours of the morning to the phone ringing. Initially, she thought she had dreamed of the ringing. When she reached for the phone all she heard was a dial tone.

Unable to fall asleep, she turned on the television. Henry's snoring agitating her, she got out of bed. Downstairs next to her daughter's favorite chair resting on the solid oak table beside it in the living room was her salvation.

She picked up the bible, closed her eyes and opened it. The passage revealed was the 23rd Psalms. Verse four slapped her hard. *Ye, though I walk through the valley of the shadow of death, I will fear no evil: For You are with me: Your rod and Your staff, they comfort me.*

The hairs on the back of her neck stood. There were goose bumps forming down her arms. She began to scratch. Alicia closed her eyes. A startling vision dropped her to her knees. Tears rolled down her face. The phone rang. Hesitantly on the third ring she grabbed the receiver.

"I know. What happened?" Grandma Alicia listened carefully to the details being given on the other end. "What!" She interrupted. "I'm sorry, continue," she said.

Grandma Alicia returned the phone receiver to its cradle. She went into the kitchen. Looking around, she started rearranging. Talking to herself she said, "The spices belong over the stove, not in some rotating shelf beside the sink. I think the lids should be in this area and the pots and pans over there."

Henry was awakened by the racket. He descends the stairs taking in the view of his daughter's beautiful home. He marvels at the plush light beige carpet his feet sink into as he winds down the stairs. The living room is elegant with its dark tan and mahogany wood Queen Anne furnishings. The formal dining room is decorated with a solid oak eight seat table. There's a matching China cabinet and hutch. He enters the kitchen to find Alicia rearranging what used to be an immaculate kitchen.

Before speaking he takes in the sight. An island sits in the middle of the floor. The cabinets are oak with stenciled glass displaying expensive dinnerware. The design on the glass is identical to the China cabinet doors in the dining room. The breakfast nook overlooks the professionally manicured backyard.

"Ya momma didn't teach you to say good morning?" Alicia says, interrupting Henry's admiration of his daughter's home.

"Good morning," Why are you rearranging this child's things? I think you enjoy antagonizing Ann. Alicia you can't do this." Henry tried reasoning with his wife. "Put her things back where she had them," he said.

"She won't need them," Alicia continued setting up her daughter's kitchen. She offered Henry a cup of coffee, finished setting up the kitchen and began preparing a hardy breakfast.

The sun was shining brightly through the beautiful bay windows. Breakfast had the entire house smelling beautifully. A quiet peaceful day was dawning. Grandpa was determined to not let Alicia ruin his.

Carl was awakened to Charles' screaming. He rushed to his crib. He changed his diaper, gave him his bottle and held him in his arms. He wouldn't stop wailing.

Caroline heard the noise. Upon entering her old room she said, "The walls were pink not blue, the crib white, not this ugly brown. Strawberry Shortcake decorated the wall border not the stupid baseball, basket ball, football and hockey stick border with that stupid mobile hanging from the crib to match." She turned to leave the room.

"Help," Carl said. "I don't know what's wrong with him. Go get Grandpa or something," he demanded.

Caroline grinned. She leisurely strolled down steps she normally took two at a time. Casually entering the kitchen, she told the Grandparents, "That baby is acting up again, think you can do something."

Alicia continued preparing breakfast ignoring her grandchild. Henry shakes his head side to side as he makes his way up the stairs.

"Okay, Okay. It's alright. I'm here now." Charles continued wailing. Grandpa Henry asked, "Has he been changed, maybe he's hungry?"   The three, Charles being carried by Grandpa, Carl holding his free hand headed down stairs.

Carl sensed something was wrong.   The gnawing feeling in his gut made him uneasy.   He held on tight to his Grandpa.

Grandma Alicia stared at the howling baby.   She approached Grandpa Henry.   "Give him to me."   He bent over to place Charles in her arms.   Grandma Alicia and her grandson's eyes locked.   He quieted.

She asked Carl to wipe down Charles' high chair as she set the dining room table.   Carl told her, "We eat breakfast in here," he said pointing to the built in breakfast nook.   She ignored him continuing to place breakfast in the center of the dining room table.

As she finished setting the table, she called for the grandchildren and Henry.   Grandma Alicia explained the rules.   "When you are called for breakfast, lunch or dinner, it will be in here. You are to thank God for receiving the blessing of food. You are not to eat or drink before grace is completed. You are not to leave the table without asking to be excused."

Caroline and Carl's eyes met. Carl couldn't shake the eerie feeling. Caroline was unusually quiet. Her lips thinned, an evil glare watched her Grandmother.

Grandma Alicia continued on with the rules. She lowered her head, raised her joined hands inches from her face and closed her eyes. *Lord we come to thank you for this nourishment. We ask that it does what you intend. That it keeps us healthy provides us with strength. Thank you for blessing us with these children. Help us guide them in the path of righteousness. As we embark on this journey of raising them, we ask for strength and courage to go forward.*

She became quiet. Carl, Caroline and Grandpa Henry all opened there eyes. Grandma Alicia continued.

Help these babies deal with the loss of there

parents, Jesus' name, amen.

The days that followed seemed to take place in slow

motion. Swarms of church goers were in attendance. The

food seemed to never stop coming. Neighbors stopped by

to pay their respect. Everyone hugged, kissed and assured

the children they would be okay.

Charles wailed through the whole service. Carl was

inconsolable, his wailing at times drowning the sound of

his brother. Caroline stared. A far away glazed expression,

she never shed a tear.

Grandpa prayed for the peaceful rest of the living

children's soul, the deliverance of the souls of Ann and

Kevin, the softening of his cold heartless wife.

Kevin and Ann Grover were buried side by side in

the Grover family plot next to Kevin's parents. The going

home celebration took place on the very day they were due

to return home.

Chapter 10

Back to Business

Three years had past. Caroline showed no signs of missing her parents. She and Alicia bickered back and forth.

The boys were not as withdrawn. They were slowly coming out of their shells. Grandpa Henry needed something to get these children back to normal.

Kevin Grover had willed his trucking business to his sons. It was time Henry came out of retirement. He felt the best way to show the boys how to become hard working upstanding citizens was by example.

He went out back and checked out the rig. Henry smiled at the memory of hitting the road, reminiscing of his days as a truck driver. He planned on working part time.

The scheduling of deliveries was made easy. Kevin was so well liked with an excellent work history. All of his patrons were willing to have Grandpa Henry continue on with their deliveries.

The plan was to leave for Michigan on Mondays. End his route in New York Wednesdays. Thursdays were for the drive back home. The rest of the week, he would be home preparing. He needed the entire family involved in the business.

A family meeting was called in the back yard. Grandpa Henry placed the punch bowl on the center of the white picnic bench. Alicia had shown Caroline how to bake oatmeal cookies which were also present for the meeting.

"Here ye, Here Ye," Grandpa says, "This meeting of the Grover- Brooks union is called to order." He spoke in a melodramatic tone. His normal Barry White tone more exaggerated.

The boys were laughing, enjoying the scene. Caroline and Grandma both wore scowls.

"Can we just get on with it," Grandma Alicia interjected.

With her eyes rolling, smacking her lips Caroline said, "Just spit it out! I don't have time for theatrics. Just get to the point. Please?"

Henry ignored the ladies directing his thoughts and concerns to his grandsons. "Your dad willed the family business to you. I thought we could all keep his legacy alive. What do you think about going into business? The women can prepare shipments. We can load and deliver.

One thing though, we all got to do are part. You three will split the profits three ways."

. "Idiot, there's five of us out here. Who do you propose should work for free?" Grandma Alicia said.

"Okay, we can split it four ways," Grandpa Henry suggested. "I will forgo my salary. The business belongs to the children. I think they should be part of keeping it alive."

It was easier to ignore Alicia's comments and continue with the task at hand. The bible says *be slow to anger.* Henry was a devoted Christian man living by that rule.

Carl and Charles had suggestions on how the business should be run. They were having a lively conversation with their Grandpa. Alicia and Caroline looked on.

"That's all wrong." Caroline gave her input. She knocked down every possible avenue of getting started.

"Grandma and I will be in charge of packaging. Carl and Charles will be laborers. You will drive the truck. It's not rocket science you know."

Her sarcasm didn't go unnoticed. Henry asked that she not speak to him in such tones. Alicia came to his aid.

Her gravelly voice was rougher than usual. Those piercing black eyes threatening, "Caroline, in this house respect is demanded. I don't know what cha momma put up with. I ain't gone stand for it, understand?" Grandma said.

Caroline stared at her grandmother one eye brow raised. She looked around before speaking "Who are you talking to? My house. My truck. My rules. You don't scare me," she continued. Mean words being thrown about at will.

Mid sentence, as Caroline was saying, "Think you gone tell me how to run my own business...," Alicia turned her tiny frame to face Caroline. Grandma Alicia's fist

connected with her mouth before another foul word was

muttered.

The boys gasped. Grandpa Henry dropped his head.

Caroline rose from the table with fury.

Grandma's fury was unmatched. She stood in

Caroline's face. "I didn't ask for this. Damned devils

reeking havoc in my life. If it were up to me, your asses

would be in foster care. I told ya momma not to be naming

me as a damned guardian to the spawn of Satan!"

As Grandma ranted no one made eye contact. The

boys were nervously eating cookies. Grandpa was wiping

the spilled punch from the picnic table. Caroline and

Grandma Alicia was matching wit word for word.

Tired of the fussing. Henry heads for the finished

basement. He liked sitting in Kevin's old beat up black

leather recliner. Grandpa turned the television to the *Gospel*

Hour show.

Carl followed. He sat himself in his mother's not so weathered matching recliner beside his Grandfather. He blankly stared at the screen of the floor model television.

Charles liked to be alone after watching the continuous sparring matches of Grandma and Caroline. Early on he took to hiding in the shed at family outbursts. Sometimes he would ease away in the middle of the verbal attacks launched at all but him by Grandma Alicia.

In the beginning no one knew where to look. Three years later it was known he spent the majority of his day there by himself.

Night falls and all is quiet in the house. Grandpa sends Carl to the shed. He walks by his squabbling grandmother and sister. They don't notice.

Inside the shed he's unable to see Charles. He flicked on the lights. "Charles, are you in here." Carl stood yelling, listening to the echo of his voice. "Grandpa says its

time for bed. You got to come in."

Charles sneaks up behind him. "Boo." He doubles

over laughing at Carl's reaction. The brothers run around

playing in the huge open space. The shed is painted white

outside with black trim to match the house. The inside is

natural wood. To the left is empty except for old dirty

covers, tires and tools placed on built in shelves. The right

side houses the eighteen wheeler delivery truck.

"We should do this family business thing." Charles

says. He turns and walks toward the back door of the

house.

Carl looks around the shed. He kicks some old

tires. He moves some old covers. He looks at the floor

boards. They appear uneven. After a brief stay in the shed,

he turns off the lights and heads back to the house.

Morning dawned. The boys were greeted by the

girls with a pleasant good morning. There singing

hymnals, finishing up with breakfast. The table is set and

they have decided the Grover- Brooks family is back in

business.

Chapter 11

The Routine

Henry was a Godsend. The children running the family business was a huge success. Days had turned into months, months into years. The Grover-Brooks clan had been together for nine years. It took a while before his eldest grandson let him in his heart.

Now Grandpa Henry is his good friend. Carl refused to give Henry the title of best friend and explained to Henry how he arrived at the title of good friend.

Carl was sixteen years old. He had grown like a weed. He was not the same cute skinny little bug eyed boy. He was now a lean handsome young man. His big dreamy brown eyes were hypnotizing. Facial hairs were appearing above his lip. His dark skin was smooth and creamy.

After Carl lost his parents, he wouldn't talk to anybody. He would be cordial but never held a conversation with substance. In a room filled with people he would intentionally go unnoticed. Now he was a sponge. He had a desire to learn everything.

Henry was outback shooting wild rabbits with a bb gun. "Hey, Grandpa, I'd like to try that? I've never shot a gun. I see you out here for hours on end, can you teach me? My dad used to say I'm real smart. I can catch on to anything. I'm sixteen now, in two years I'll be a grown man and I know I'm ready." Carl said.

Henry laughed while he waited for an opening. "Okay, Okay already, I was never gone tell my favorite grandson no," Henry said with a grin and wink of his eye.

Carl smiled back broadly. "I am your favorite grandson? That's great because you're my favorite grandparent. You can't tell Grandma Alicia though and I won't tell Charles. Guess what else, you're my good friend," Carl announced beaming with pride. "Daddy was my best friend but you okay too. How 'bout that ole man," Carl said laughing.

Grandpa Henry was thrilled. "You know I don't know who you think you calling ole man," he said. "This ole man can still take a young whipper snapper like your tall bony behind. And let me tell you something else, last one to the shed cleans up after we get done."

Grandpa Henry was walking and talking giving himself a lead. Both ran to the shed and were cracking up laughing.

Carl let his grandfather win with pride. He deliberately pretended to be out of breath and barely making it inches behind.

Henry had Carl collect tin cans for target practice. He sat Carl down and explained how dangerous guns were in the wrong hands. He explained what their use was for and how to be extremely careful.

Henry was so pleased with himself. He felt he had finally broken down that wall Carl had put up around his heart. The only people with access were his siblings.

The two made a date to meet after school on occasion until Carl became an expert not needing supervision.

Carl had become accustomed to helping Grandpa Henry with deliveries. Henry beamed with pride of his grandson's after school dedication to the family business.

Carl became bored. He mentioned his feelings to his grandfather. "Grandpa I don't want to spend my life doing this. This was my dad's dream. I got my own aspirations. I want to go to college and maybe become a writer," he said.

"You know I've been writing my thoughts and memories since I was seven. There is nine years of my thoughts written down. I might want to publish it one day as a memoir to my parents."

Henry looked over at his eldest grandson and then at Charles. Carl's smooth dark skin was breath taking. He had the chiseled features of a male model. Charles caramel complexion matched his sister's. His brown eyes were sad. There was no strong family resemblance between the two.

Charles never had much to say. He was always watching. He'd watch everything from how the truck was loaded and unloaded to how the birds perched in the yard. He never initiated a conversation, just one word answers when Grandpa tried to engage him. If asked how are you? The response would be "fine," If asked are you hungry? The answer was always "yes."

Carl went on and on about his career and dedication of writing a memoir. Henry interrupted by asking Charles, "What you think about your brother becoming some big time book writer?"

Charles response was, "okay."

Carl looked back and forth between his grandfather and little brother. Grandpa always encouraged Charles to speak or participate. He gave the baby boy his undivided attention at all times.

Chapter 12

The Baby Boy

Charles was distant. Kevin and Ann weren't allotted enough time to nurture him was the consensus of the adults in his life. Suspicion lurked about his character, he never made eye contact.

Early on Carl and Caroline would ask what happened to their parents. The grandparents would clam up.

The answer given was, "She was here for a short while. God called her home with her husband," Grandma Alicia would say. Grandpa Henry wouldn't answer. Charles listened intently.

He had decided that somehow Henry and Alicia were responsible for his parents' death.

When no one was looking Charles would read his brother's journals. He'd pretend that he had known the parents as well as his big brother.

He wanted to let Carl know he was thankful. He was keeping the parents alive through the writings. They made these two strangers real for him.

He wasn't so happy about the entries he read concerning Caroline but was unsure of how to approach the subject. The entry in question read: *Mommy if you were alive today you would be so proud of how Caroline turned out. She looks like you and through me and daddy's prayers she's no longer evil. She attends church and quotes scripture with Grandma Alicia all the time. I never told you about what dad and I were discussing in the truck. By now I know you discussed it together in heaven. She has changed now, she either doesn't remember it or don't*

care to discuss it. I still can't sit in her room if it's just the

two of us at home. I make sure we are always within

earshot of Charles or the grandparents. I haven't forgotten

but I have forgiven. You can't blame a boy for being

careful. My best friend taught me that.

Ps, I'll write some more later on. As always goodnight

and I love you both.

"Why does he refer to them as 'the grandparents?'
What did Caroline do, when was she ever evil, how come
nobody ever tells me anything?" Charles said.

As he was speaking Carl walked in laughing.

"What's up, what do you want to know," Carl said
intrigued by the confused look on Charles' face.

"I want to know what Caroline did and why you say
she's evil, "Charles responded.

"I know you ain't been snooping through my things.
I just know you haven't. Carl berated his little brother. "I

trusted you and you betrayed me! If you wanted to know anything all you had to do is ask. I have never hid anything from you before. Anytime you ask me something I give you a straight forward answer and you pull this sh…!"

Grandpa Henry heard all the yelling. He came rushing into the room.

Charles began to cry and ran to his grandfather. "I think he was going to hit me Grandpa."

"And what were you going to do if he had?" Grandpa Henry chuckled.

"I was going to hit him back and tell." Charles confessed.

He looked Carl in the eye. "Were you going to hit your little brother?" Grandpa Henry asked.

"No. I just wanted him to know that he can't read other peoples stuff and think its okay.   It's a violation of privacy," he yelled.

"Didn't you tell us you wanted to publish it as a tribute to your parents," Grandpa asked.

"Yes but you didn't think I could or at least you didn't encourage me to do it."

"So," Grandpa interrupted Carl. "You're impatient and you little man is nosy. You Carl, if don't nobody answer you right away you get bent out of shape. You Charles sneak around listening to folks and sneaking through their things but don't talk to nobody. We leave you alone, you get mad. I'm gone close this door and you boys are gone hash this out like men. Real men don't scream, yell or punch either out." Grandpa Henry listened at the door.

"Okay what you read wasn't my tribute it was my diary and that's messed up. If I can't trust my brother, you tell me who I can trust?" Carl said.

"Look, I'm not a kid anymore. I am eleven years old. You still treat me like a two year old. You won't let me lift the big boxes at work. You won't sit down and talk to me man to man. I'm tired of this baby crap. I know I'm the youngest sibling but you got to cut me some slack. This baby crap is getting old," Charles said.

"Oh, so you a big man now? Don't need your brother looking out for you. Is that what you're saying?"

"No, I look for you to let me know you are there when I need you but I don't need you all the time." Charles reasoned.

"Okay we got an understanding. I will leave you alone until you need me. But sometimes I may step in when you think you don't need me but you do."

"Carl, I bet Daddy used to say stuff like that to you," Charles said lowering his head.

Carl realized the advantage he and Caroline had over their brother. He was a baby when his life changed.

He looked at his brother for a minute. Carl went to his room. He returned with a composition note book.

"Look here man, if you want to read my journal that's okay. My diaries you flat out can't read. Come on shake my hand man, let's squash this," Carl said extending his right hand.

Charles and Carl shook hands. Carl handed his brother the first journal he had written. He left his brother's room with his head bowed.

Chapter 13

Discovery

After the truck was loaded, dinner was served, everyone went their separate ways. Charles followed Grandpa Henry to the back of the house.

In the presence of the grandparents he didn't speak much. He played on his grandfather's heartstrings that were becoming more and more attached.

The only way Grandpa knew to show someone the way was to lead them to the Lord. He took Charles to every church meeting loading him up on the youth programs.

He knew his grandson to be straight forward. The one

word answers supplied were honest. Everyone else warned

of watching out for the quiet ones.   He was approached by

a fellow elder of the church. "Deacon Brooks, you got a

minute?" That old trouble maker Deacon Smith was asking.

Grandpa Henry was trying to avoid him

inconspicuously. He had seen Smith manipulate stories to

fit his version of events on several occasions. Being a

church man and all, Henry knew he was trapped. He

couldn't be rude to Deacon Smith. If he had it would

surely be mentioned in Sunday's sermon by Reverend

Cole.

"Hey there Deacon Smith, God is good isn't he?

You know it. Done blessed me with three youngsters after

all this time. What can I help you with?"

"Yes, God is good" Deacon Smith responded. "I need to talk to you outside of earshot of this here fine young man Brother Brooks."

"Okay, Charles, go on over to the truck. You know we got to get home before Grandma Alicia sends the sheriff out looking for us," he winked at his grandson.

Charles went to the truck and rolled the window down. He knew Deacon Smith was not good at keeping his voice low.

"Now Brooks we are both upstanding members of this church. I consider you to be a friend. I think God laid this burden on my heart because of our friendship. I am going to just tell you what some of the nurses say they saw. They claim that youngest boy you got with you tonight..."

Grandpa Henry interrupted, "that boy's name is Charles Grover."

Deacon Smith continued. "Sorry, didn't mean anything by it, just getting old and forgetful. Anyways the nurses say he and the girl, I mean Caroline were the last two observed at the youth dance by the collection plate. Sister Harris said she had counted the money, got a call, closed the lid and went and took that call. When she came back that basket was about twenty five dollars short. No they didn't come right out and say it was the boy, I mean Charles."

Deacon Smith looked directly into Grandpa Henry's eyes eagerly awaiting a denial. A slip of the tongue. Something that would make good gossip for Sunday morning services.

Grandpa Henry politely through an angered smile. He thanked Deacon Smith for being such a 'good friend.' He informed him neither of his children were thieves.

He went on to say, "Charles is about the most

squeamish little fellow I know, he don't talk much. He is

very jumpy after losing his parents.   I would think a bunch

of Christian folk would know better than to accuse an

innocent child of thievery. Charles is already having a hard

time. You people want to accuse him of some crap like

this!"

Grandpa Henry excused himself and proceeded to

walk to his car where his little buddy Charles had dozed

off. "Im grateful that he didn't over hear any of that

nonsense," he said slamming the car into drive.

As they pulled into the driveway he nudged

Charles awake. With the truck parked in the garage, he

looked over at the shed. The lights must have been left on

by Charles.

"Charles turn out those lights," Grandpa said.

Charles enters the shed to find Carl and Caroline

huddled up. In unison they scramble to cover up some

papers.

"What's going on?" Charles asked.

"We found some interesting papers and stuff in the floorboards over there. Caroline and I need to figure them out. When we do, we'll fill you in later. Charles, this has to be kept between the three of us." Carl said.

Charles in a hushed tone suggested they put them back. He informed them that Grandpa was right outside. "We will meet after school when are chores are completed and discuss it tomorrow," he suggested.

Carl was fine with the meeting. He told his little brother it was a great idea. Caroline smiled making him feel uneasy in his own skin.

After wondering what was taking so long for Charles to return to the car, Grandpa headed toward the shed.

"Surprise!" Caroline screamed catching Henry off guard. He stumbled around before gaining his balance.

"We are camping out here tonight. You're invited," she said.

Carl was thankful Caroline was quick on her feet. Charles later told his sister she was a master mind. Grandpa Henry wondered what they were up to.

For the next several months they brushed off friends, rushed through chores, half done packaging and loading the truck. They stayed in the shed until called to dinner.

Charles was always first to arrive most days. His chores were minimal in comparison to his siblings. He'd hang around inside the house waiting for Caroline and Carl to complete their responsibilities.

On occasion Grandma Alicia and he would have conversations. If he wasn't with Alicia, he followed Grandpa around until his siblings finished their chores.

Chapter 14

Growing Pangs

Caroline seems to have changed the most. She and Grandma Alicia appear to be gal pals. She's learning to cook and clean to Alicia's standards.

Caroline at fourteen was already as beautiful as her mother. She was tall and slender. Her eyes were a beautiful bright brown, complimenting her perfect coffee with cream colored complexion. She had legs like Tina Turner and knew it. She only wore skirts. She flaunted her good looks at school. She made attempts to gain Grandpa's attention as well.

Alicia was thrilled. It was like God had sent her daughter back. This time mother and daughter loved each other and were the best of friends. She wanted to mold Caroline into the young lady Ann refused to be.

The pair spent hours in the house preparing for shipments, cleaning, cooking and talking from the time Caroline returned from school.

Caroline would address the family every morning, "Good Morning Family, love you all from the top of my head to the bottom of my soles, but you know I love God more."

Alicia was quite pleased. She would tell Henry "God's given us a second chance to get it right. He sent us those three precious children of our only child and they've been a blessing. Things are changing for the better 'round here Henry."

Henry noted how happy Alicia was. He was not as easily fooled by the pretty little girl trying to wrap them around her sneaky little fingers.

Henry had witnessed Caroline being nasty to Charles. They had been with them around five years at the time. She was ten years old. He was speaking appropriately for a seven year old. It was more than sibling rivalry. It was cruelty.

Caroline was ragging on Charles' speech. She called him a retard. Suggested they would never get out of this sad situation. She said Grandpa Henry and Grandma Alicia were both crazy old coots.

Caroline ranted about taking take the grandparents for everything they were worth. She accused them of stealing the trucking business, said they were putting on a holier than thou act.

She told Charles stealing is one of the Ten Commandments not to be broken. The punishment is eternal damnation. Even suggested helping God out by setting the fire.

Caroline scared Charles so badly. He refused to go to church the next Sunday. He begged his grandparents to stay home.

Henry never told Alicia what he heard. The woman was smitten with getting her reincarnated daughter back.

He approached Caroline's bedroom. Her door was ajar. He glared at her and turned away.

He went out in the yard. Caroline followed. She jumped up, hugged his legs and started thanking him for bringing her into his life.

Sunday rolled around and Caroline said she was going to have church at home. Said she had cramps so bad she couldn't get out of bed. She quoted scripture to Alicia. *For where two or three are gathered together in My name,*

I am there among them. She begged Alicia to let the boys

stay home. Alicia was so happy and taken in by this

beautiful child. After that Oscar worthy performance

Grandma Alicia agreed. The plan was set in motion and

working smoothly.

Henry sternly looked deep into her eyes, "There are

to be no fires set," he whispered.

Caroline was astonished.   Evilness lurked behind

her smile. She decided she would go to church after all.

She walked up to Alicia, dressed in her lavender short

fitting dress. Her beautiful long black hair pulled back in a

French roll. She was doubled over from the pain of

imaginary cramps.

Caroline went for the academy award. "Grandma,

if God can give his only begotten son so that I may be

given life, I can bear the pain and go to church."

Because of Caroline's performance there trip to

church was shorter than usual. No one attended Sunday

school. They made it to the church just as devotion was

ending and the service was to start.

The boys were grateful. Alicia was peeved. She

was placing blame on Henry. "Henry, I have told you, I

don't want any more devils in my house. You have got to

stop scaring this girl so bad. She won't come within fifteen

feet of you. It's just not right. Now I done missed Sunday

school because of your heathen ways," Alicia said.

Henry wasn't enjoying the sermon. "I know she is

not chastising me. A grown man in church! How dare she

blame me for missing Sunday school," he mumbled under

his breath before praying. *God if you just give her the*

strength to see through this demon we inherited and help us

make her whole. I ask You please let today be the day you

drive the demon out of this child, in Jesus name, amen.

Caroline was sitting between Alicia and Henry. After completion of his silent prayer he looked over to see Caroline grinning.

From that day on Henry kept an eye on Caroline at all times. He continued to pray for her soul in silence and would not let her cold grinning stare distract him.

Alicia was following along with the sermon, praising the lord. She was oblivious to what was happening next to her.

Charles noticed there was tension between Caroline and Grandpa Henry. He tugged on Carl's suit jacket. "I need to go to the bathroom," he said.

As Henry had taken to babying Charles, it was routine for Carl to escort him.

Carl had a sixth-sense when it came to his little brother. He knew when he wanted to talk. It wasn't that often. They waited on a break in the 'beware of devils

wearing sheep clothing' sermon.

In the bathroom, Charles was acting suspicious. He

waited for the gentleman using the urinal to wash his hands

and leave. He looked under stalls. Charles began an

interesting conversation with his big brother.

"Man, something is going on with Grandpa and

Caroline. You've been telling me since I can remember

you are the leader of the family. Well I think you need to

step in. Ask Grandpa Henry why he hates Caroline. We

know she's different but I feel like he's trying to change

her. I don't want her to change. She is scary sometimes

but that's okay. We are all a little different," Charles said.

Carl was not following Charles. It was sometimes

hard to follow him when he rarely spoke. On the few

occasions he did talk in length Carl found himself listening to the sound of his voice. He knew Charles hated to repeat himself. He asked him to slow down and explain.

"You weren't listening man." Charles spoke loud and clear. "Grandpa Henry hates Caroline. I think he is asking God to change her. We all know Caroline is mean. She is my mother, I mean sister and I don't want her to change. Grandpa Henry wants her to be like every one else. We got to love her for whom she is," he said.

Charles was speaking clearly. Carl wasn't following. Everyone seemed happy to him. Especially Alicia and Caroline. They seemed closer than she and their mother Ann had ever been.

"Charles, I think you are overreacting. You don't know what Grandpa Henry is praying for when he prays in silence. He doesn't hate Caroline. I need you to give me some specifics on what you may have overheard or saw that I might be able to explain it away," Carl said.

"Carl, I don't need you to 'explain away' nothing

for me. I am not a baby, I know what I've seen and I know

what I've heard. You've pulled away from Caroline

because she looks like momma. You and Grandpa Henry

are working together to make her feel like an outsider.

You're supposed to be the leader but you don't listen. You

don't see. You are full of crap!" Charles stated. He

stormed out of the bathroom returning to his seat.

Chapter 15

Breakdown in Communications

Grandpa hadn't said anything about Carl

going to college. Caroline was mimicking Grandma Alicia.

Charles talked more. Not a lot but more than yes and no

answers.

Grandpa prayed for all of them. He usually saved

Caroline for the end. He prayed '*Lord if you just give*

Alicia the wisdom to see this child don't love her, this child

don't love anybody. She's the devil reincarnated to look

just like our Ann. The One who sows the good seed is the

Son of Man; the field is the world; and the good seed--these are the sons of the kingdom. The weeds are the sons of the

evil one, and the enemy who sowed them is the Devil.'

Grandpa continued praying. *We know you took Ann from*

us as soon as she became pure and we know that the devil

was spawn again through Caroline. I pray that you save

her soul and give us the strength to teach her your

ways. God please give us the strength to wrestle with the

demon in this child. Know that I am trying. In Jesus' name

amen."

Chapter 16

School Daze

Carl was sitting in his last period math class unable
to concentrate. He had started to notice the distance
between his grandfather and Caroline.

He was dismissed a few minutes early from school
and hung around with his friends waiting on Caroline to be
dismissed. As he waited he recalled the last time spent in
the old truck with his dad.

. Carl started telling his daddy everything. His
sister had told his dad he was trying to molest her. Kevin
had taken him out to the truck

"Daddy, that's sick. Something is wrong with her. I can't stand her half the time. The other half I wish she was dead! You got to believe me, I did not touch her. I haven't touched anybody. I think she's crazy! I know she is." Carl cried.

Kevin let him get it all out of his system before speaking. "I know you didn't touch your sister. Nobody has touched your sister but the enemy of God. You are absolutely correct. Between you and me, man to man, I can tell you something without you repeating it? I have been trying to get your mother to see Caroline is disturbed. She is full of hate and envy. Only Satan could make someone like her. It happened with your grandmother on your momma's side of the family. She was the seventh female born. . Old wise folk say you can't have seven girls born first in each generation. They say the seventh will be the devil's offspring. Your grandmother hides behind that bible. She's a snake in sheep's clothing. "

Carl sat behind the wheel of the truck shaking uncontrollably. He looked out the window glad to see his mother approaching the truck. His reliving that horrific event was interrupted by his sister's current actions.

Caroline exited the schoolhouse arm and arm with a boy. They were about the same height. He was the brown of the crayon. His eyes were the color and shape of an almond. This boy wasn't chubby but thin wouldn't be an accurate description. Caroline might have been an inch taller.

When she spotted Carl she quickly snatched her arm away. A look of embarrassment followed by blushing clouded Caroline's eyes.

Carl rushed right over and spoke to the young man. "Hey man, my name is Carl Grover," he said extending his hand. "How are you?"

"I'm fine, my name is Brandon James. Nice to meet you man. No need to get bent out of shape 'cause I'm with your sister and all. She told me so much about you I

feel I already know you Carl Grover."

"Brandon I haven't heard a thing about you. That

sound's like a good idea you and me getting to know each

other. Today ain't a good day. We got to go pick up my

little brother Charles. I'm sure you heard about him too,"

Carl said as he was retrieving Caroline's books from

Brandon.

"Caroline what in the hell is going on? I just know

you had better not told that boy anything about our family.

He's not one of us, he's not a Grover. The three of us is all

we have. If I can't trust you, Charles and I will have to

leave you behind. Ever since we figured out those papers

in the shed, you've been flaky. Didn't I tell you we are

going to take the money our parents left and leave," he

asked. "I think the only reason they haven't said a word

about my money is so they can spend it on themselves!

Whatever they haven't spent on by twentieth birthday is

mine. They named me as guardian of Charles and you.

I'm in my last year of school. We don't have long," he said

Carl's nostrils flared as he spoke. His hands were

flailing about. "We have a little less than three years to get

the hell out of here. I ain't taking any extra baggage!"

Caroline had that scary grin on her face. "You ain't

my daddy. He was killed by your grandfather!" She

watched Carl's reaction before continuing. "Yes you heard

me. I've been doing some digging of my own. Old man

Henry ain't the saint you want him to be," she said.

Her piercing eyes betraying a rage unleashed

thumping her temples. "Oh I have been watching you.

Always working and talking to him and shit. Your dumb

ass is being treated like the staff and you own the property.

But me and Charles, we got to find our own way. Momma saw fit that you be given the title of favorite child and reaping the benefits of her death."

It was weird. Caroline and Ann, mother and daughter had the same eyes. The eyes were beautiful on Ann, scary on Caroline. Yet the same eyes.

"He killed your momma too, fool! Grandma's been talking a whole lot. She blamed it on them fevers she claim to be getting. 'Talking about she needs to go lay down. Leaving me to cook and clean and service her husband. Hell the whole lot of you make me sick to my stomach!"

Carl watched Caroline trembling and shaking, smiling while revealing all of this information. Tears were streaming down her cheeks.

"You thought I was lying the first time I told you about Grandpa didn't you? Admit it, you did. I saw it in your eyes. Not once did you come to my room when I asked. You let me fend for myself. What did your precious granddaddy tell you about that new scar on his head, told you he ran into the shed again right?"

Carl had notice the scar that morning. Grandpa told him he got it delivering. He said the door hinges on the delivery truck had rusted through. His Grandpa asked him to assist in replacing the hinges. He continued listening to his sister.

"That is not how he got it. He got it by me taking a piece of that wood out back, hiding it under my bed and slapping the shit out of him!. Oh and your holy sanctified on my way to heaven grandmother, she rushed into the room. She saw all the commotion turned around and walked out, chanting," Caroline paused. "Something to the Lord about '*no, not again' over and over again she said*. Your granddaddy lay beside that bed for minutes unconscious with his pants at his ankles."

Saddened by his sister's actions. Carl walked with his head bowed. He silently prayed for her demonic soul. Caroline wasn't done yet.

"I followed Alicia around the house listening, numb," she said. She began mocking her grandmother's prayer. *'Lord you sent my daughter back for this monster to take her away from me too! Lord Jesus no, please stop the pain. What have I done to deserve this? Lord Jesus knows I can't take no more. I follow all your rules. I stand by this man as you say and yet he has taken my daughter and now her replacement. Please Lord show me the way.'*

Carl hugged Caroline tightly as tears fell down his face. They walked in silence.

One could only imagine if things would have been different for Caroline had Kevin lived. He was the only person that didn't fall for her mess. Kevin ignored her mostly. She tried on several occasions to get under his skin.

Kevin had once held a cross he wore around his neck up to her. Caroline smiled and said "that is no match for me."

Ann asked "what was that honey?" Caroline said "nothing."

Chapter 17

The Scheme of Things

As they approached Charles' school, Carl abruptly stopped. He cleaned Caroline's face, then his own. "Caroline does anyone else no about this." Caroline shook her head.

They approached Charles with phony smiles. The three of them walked toward the bus stop in silence.

"Hey what happened, why are you two so quiet today, what is Caroline lying about now?" Charles fired off questions expecting an answer from Carl.

Charles hadn't told Carl about the secret meetings he and Caroline had. He was unsure if he could trust either of his siblings. He had to tell someone quick before she put her plan in motion.

Caroline had been suggesting to Charles that Carl was going to turn on them. She almost had Charles convinced that it was Carl tearing the three of them apart. She was telling Charles that Carl was going to go away to college. He would take the money Ann left and forget they were left behind. She and Charles would remain slaves working their own land.

"He'll be some fancy writer who pretends he was born rich and didn't have any siblings. Can't you just see him in his big house and fancy clothes? He'll probably marry some holy roller like Grandma Alicia. He's always talking about how we can't tell you everything because you aren't that smart Charles. That will be his reason for leaving you. His reason for leaving me will be he can't face his failure for not saving me from Grandpa," Caroline said.

She tried to convince him that their meetings had to be kept quiet. "He has already told me he would kill you. He and I would go down south,"Caroline said.

Carl tried unsuccessfully to tell his little brother nothing was wrong.

"Bullshit, the both of you have been crying. Now you come to get me with them phony ass smiles treating me like I'm some young ass child who don't know what the f..."

Carl cut him off before he could finish. "What is your problem using that language? I don't know where you learned it from but it's unacceptable. Talk like that makes you look ignorant," he said.

"While you think you got every thing all figured out, let me enlighten you. Caroline has a boyfriend his name is Brandon. She says Grandpa Henry is inappropriately touching her and a whole bunch of other stuff. I don't want to go into it until we get home. So look here Mr. Big man that knows a few bad words you shut up until we get home or I will shut you up!" Carl demanded.

Carl, Caroline and Charles walked to the bus stop in complete silence. Neither child looked at the other. The three of them stared straight ahead with grim looks on their faces.

The school bus pulled up. The driver asked the three of them to wait on the curb. He was a short balding fat white man that everyone loved. He asked, "Is everything okay with you guys? Please tell me no one else has died. You three have had enough."

He looked to Caroline. She was smiling. Charles looked surprised. He turned to Carl.

"Mr. Lewis, no one has passed away to our knowledge. We are getting along just fine. Thank you for your concern but we would like to board the bus," Carl informed the driver.

"Well I'm sorry Carl the three of you just looked awful sad. If I could have helped I would. Your momma and daddy were great people, good friends of mine. They would never forgive me if they looked down from the heavens and saw that I wasn't doing what I could for their babies. Now I know you didn't want me asking in front of them idiots," Mr. Lewis asked pointing back to the bus.

"No sir, I appreciate your candor but there is nothing wrong. We would like to get home," Carl stated with a smile that seemed to put Mr. Lewis at ease.

"Well alright then what are you three holding up my route for? Get your behinds on the bus." All four smiled and took their usual places for the long ride home.

Chapter 18

Meeting of Minds

The bus ride seemed longer. Carl and Charles were discreetly watching Caroline. Caroline stared straight ahead.

As soon as the bus pulled to their stop, the three Grover children leaped off and walked up hill quickly. The school uniforms were taken off in a hurry, the play clothes were put on. The shipment preparations hurried through, chores were done at lightening speed. Off they went to the shed.

As usual Carl spoke first. "Let's quit all the dumb stuff. Nobody is leaving this shed until all cards are face up on the table."

"You go first then." Caroline chimed in. Plastered across her face was a wicked smirk.

Normally Charles would be quiet intensely listening to the both of them bickering back and forth resolving nothing.

"I don't know that I can trust either of you. I am the youngest but I am not a baby. I hear and see more than you think. . Carl, you think you know everything. You got it all figured out. We are supposed to trust you with the money our parents left. Did you think I didn't know they split the funds three ways?" Charles paused giving time for his words to sink in.

Caroline's eyes brightened. She honed in on Carl. Carl said nothing.

"We all get a third of their estate upon our twentieth birthday. The money our grandparents are spending was allocated since each of our births and from their family insurance plan. It was done in case something happened before we were considered adults."

Charles took a long pause. He turned to his sister. "Caroline, you are a liar. You play God for your benefit. You do know you will be dealt with on judgment day right!"

Charles looked as though he was going to lash out further. Swiftly his head rotated looking from Caroline to Carl and back. Neither Carl nor Caroline knew how to react to his outbursts.

"You little two-faced punk! How dare you call me a liar after what you've done? I've been covering for you since the beginning. I'm the one that never fit in!" Caroline retorted. "Grandma Alicia and Daddy with their crazy beliefs of the seventh girl child, Momma and Carl never believing anything I say!"

Caroline stood up pacing as the floorboards squeaked under her stomping feet. She continued unleashing her feelings. "Grandma Alicia may be a Jesus freak but I love her more than she ever loved momma. She loves me. And furthermore, I don't care what you, Grandpa or Carl and our parents think. Brandon James and I are getting the hell out of Bedford Ohio as soon as I get my hands on some money. Be it what our parents left or what I find on my own. I will never ever speak to any of you again!"

Carl jumped up his nose and Caroline's inches apart. "How dare you! Our parents loved us all and you are a liar. Have you ever told our baby, oops our youngest brother the lies you made up about me? You swore I tried to molest you. Remember that. You liar! You said the same thing about Daddy. Now you are saying it about Grandpa

Henry!"

Carl was unsteady on his feet. He struggled to lower

himself to the floor. The thumping rhythm of his heart

pounding in his ear.

He took several deep breaths before continuing.

"You also swore you didn't tell anybody about the papers I

found. I guess that was a lie to 'because little brother here

seems to know all about it," he said.

Charles approached Carl. "Are you alright?"

His breathing returned to normal. He continued.

"You've embellished a little further about three trust funds,

give me a break Caroline for once have a backbone, tell the

truth. As far as this Brandon person, you don't even know

him. I am sure you haven't let him see the real you. Once

he gets a glimpse of the real you, you can forget about him

marrying a lying, conniving winch like you," Carl stated

coldly.

"Shut up. Shut up. Shut up! Charles shouted. This

isn't about Carl, this isn't about Caroline. This is about me.

I found those papers in the shed long before you Carl. I

read them. I showed them to Grandpa Henry. He assured

me that they could not touch our money. The life insurance

policy they were paid out on was more than enough.

Grandpa is not a greedy man. He's doing the right thing.

You know there is a college fund so that you can become a

writer or whatever else you decide," he said.

All three were seated on the wooden floor. The

silence in the shed was deafening. Caroline's arms folded

across her chest. Charles' head down, eyes focused on the

floorboards. Carl indiscreetly took deep breaths.

"I read about Caroline's lies in your diaries Carl. I

know you told me not to read them," Charles said. He

never raised his lowered head. "I could tell something was

missing in the journals. The whole story wasn't being told. Caroline you wonder why Grandpa despises you. Think about it. You think he killed his own child! You accused him of molesting you! You go around spitting venom at everyone in sight. If it walks like an evil duck, quacks like an evil duck, it's an evil duck," Charles yelled.

Quietness followed. Thoughts unspoken in everyone's head. Carl and Caroline looked scared of where this meeting had taken them.

"Remember the stomach flu. It was the sickness of the both of you that kept me home from school for a week." Charles said. He swallowed hard. His lips twisted up. His dark brown eyes turned black. "You make my skin crawl," he said shuddering. "I wonder if I am the lucky one for not knowing our parents as well. My observation tells me our parents weren't that great," Charles said.

The children ended the meeting. They decided to
meet up on Sunday after church. You could here a pin drop.
The Grover Children had reached the point of no return.

Carl was shocked his brother was holding back
information.

Caroline was impressed. She was proud Charles
wasn't the spineless wimp Grandma Alicia pegged him to
be. Mumbling inaudibly she said "It's about time he let
someone other than me see his true grit. It's almost funny
that I'm the one they refer to as evil. He had better not say
much more or I'll have his ass for lunch." The eerie grin
crept back upon her lips. A cold icy stare directed at
Charles.

Charles didn't notice the death glare of his sister.
Instead he focused on Carl. Underneath his breath he said
"Leader hell. Grandma and Caroline are the leaders. They

guide him around by the nose. He is so predictable. I'll give it five seconds and he will be patronizing me with the little brother I love you crap. One thousand one, one thousand two, one thousand three..."

"Okay Charles You know I love you. Maybe I wasn't forthcoming with information because you are always going to be my little brother."

Caroline and Charles' eyes met.

Carl had been snowed by the both of them. He decided to keep on talking. "Okay, from here on I am going to treat you as you deserve to be treated, not like some snot nose baby. But you got to start talking. I had no idea you were mad at me and Caroline. You can tell me how you feel. You don't need to keep secrets from me. We can share everything, I'm not mad you read my diaries. I'll admit I am hurt because I told you those were my personal thoughts. I wouldn't want to harm somebody with something that I said in the diary. That doesn't mean that's

how I really feel."

Charles smiled. "Look Carl, everybody thinks that

Caroline is mean. I think they got it wrong. The stuff you

wrote about your parents, you're truly evil."

Caroline's face lit up, her cold heartless smile

disappeared. "What did he write about our parents?"

Chapter 19

Pieces of the Puzzle

The children spent the remainder of the weekend speaking only when necessary to one another.

Right on cue at six thirty Grandma Alicia called them in for dinner. "Saved by the bell," Charles said aloud.

They took their normal seats around the dining room table, Grandma Alicia at the head, Grandpa Henry at the other end, Caroline and Charles to Alicia's right, Carl across from them.

Grandma Alicia always made big Sunday dinners. Set center of the massive table was a beautiful sterling silver roasting pan with chicken and all the trimmings. In matching silver bowls were candied yams, green beans, dinner roles. The table was loaded with everything you would expect for a holiday feast.

Grandma Alicia believed God gave his only begotten Son for us to have life. Sundays were to be celebrated. And so they did except this life shattering Sunday.

The children were in a sullen mood. Grandpa Henry was the first to break the ice. "Hey what you kids got such long faces about?"

Neither child bothered to reply.

"I know you heathens heard your grandfather ask you a question. Don't make me go around this table cracking heads before thanking God for this food!" Grandma Alicia said.

No one spoke.

"Let me tell you ungrateful little ingrates a thing or two. In this house, my house when an adult addresses you,

you give them the utmost respect. When a question is

asked you answer it. When told to speak, you do so. Now

before you let Satan loose through my tongue," Grandma

Alicia paused, "Somebody had better answer Grandpa's

question."

The children shifted nervously in their chairs. They

spoke in unison.

"Dagnabbit what is wrong with you demon seeds

today! Do I have to spell out everything? You can't speak

at once and expect to be heard. In this house lady's first,"

Grandma said, extending an invitation to Caroline.

"Okay, Grandma you want us to tell you what's

going on. Can your old battle ax of a heart take it? Call on

Jesus now before it's too late, Caroline said waving her

hands as if in church. "Once I start, I want you to shut up

and listen. You got that old bird," Caroline yelled.

"First of all, I know that your husband killed my

parents to inherit our house and family business. We were

just pawns in his evil game. I know that you didn't want us

here because you think we are possessed. Greed got the

best of you." Caroline's words drug out. She paused

between sentences. Her eyes focused on her grandmother.

"You figured we were a necessary evil for all that money."

She then placed her focus on Grandpa Henry as she

continued. She paused, turned back to lashing out at

Grandma Alicia. "I know that your husband visits my bed

at least twice a week. He's taking up where my daddy left

off!" Caroline's accusatory glare and smiling face dared

Grandpa Henry to deny it.

. "Caroline, you are sick! Grandpa Henry and

Daddy are right. You are crazy! I don't know much about

this seventh girl child crap. I do know you are not normal.

You need help spiritually and mentally," Carl yelled.

Charles didn't speak. He watched the battle of the

siblings. He shook his head when Caroline spoke, smirked

when Carl had his turn. Charles listened intently when

Grandma Alicia spoke. He rolled his eyes when Grandpa prayed.

Grandma Alicia was not fazed by her granddaughter's comments. She had overheard her fare share of conversations. She looked Caroline in the eye before speaking, her crooked smile as eerie as Caroline's.

"Look here Jezebel I noticed you haven't had your period for two months." Grandma Alicia said in a deep gruff tone. "So don't think you can play this 'old bird' for a fool," she said pointing at herself.

Caroline's smile faded. She lowered her head.

Grandma Alicia continued. "Henry ain't the one causing you to miss no monthlies. It's that little old nappy head boy. You know who I'm talking about. Henry ain't killed your parents. Wasn't his fault your cheating momma got them killed in New York!"

The children and Grandpa Henry gasped. Pandora's Box had been opened.

Grandma Alicia was just getting started. She looked to Charles. "It's time we lay all cards on the table… face up."

Carl fixated on Charles.

"Charles get me all those papers out of the shed. Bring the pictures in the box on top of the armoire in my room. It's high time we hash all this out," Grandma Alicia said.

While Charles was following his grandmother's orders, she was cleaning off the table. As she removed dishes from the table Carl tried to leave the room.

"Carl, get back here! As I stated we are going to hash this out here and now. We are going to put all this backstabbing and who shot John behind us tonight. This whole mess will be laid to rest," Grandma Alicia stated firmly.

Charles came back into the dining room with his head hanging down. He handed Grandma Alicia three manila envelopes stuffed with papers, two hat boxes filled

with pictures and a black envelope.

Caroline and Carl gawked at each other and

Charles. He refused to acknowledge their glares.

Grandpa Henry approached the head of the table.

He put his hand on top of Grandma Alicia's. "Are you sure

you want to do this. They're still babies you know. This

could break their spirits. They might not ever recover from

the shock of it all," he said.

When Grandma Alicia took the lid off the hat box

Grandpa lowered his head. His shoulders slumped. Slowly

he walked back to his seat.

She looked through pictures pulling out some.

Grandma turned them faced down on the table. She

grimaced at a few, smiled pleasantly at others. She

retrieved seven pictures before replacing the lid.

She looked over at Grandpa Henry, "It's time we

end the charade. You're either with me or against me. I

can't expect to get to heaven with the secrets and lies we keep telling ourselves are in the best interest of family," Grandma Alicia said. "You know all the commandments. The one we have been breaking for years, *thou shall not bear false witness*. We didn't start the lies. But guilty in the eyes of the Lord for perpetuating it."

The ticking of the dining room clock could be was the only sound heard.

Grandpa Henry sighed. He prayed in silence for a while. He blew a kiss to his wife before breaking the silence. "Your call, don't go blaming the Lord for what you wanted to tell," he said.

He looked at the children until all acknowledged his glance. His eyes pleaded with Grandma Alicia to stop.

Chapter 20

Family Photos

The first picture revealed was of Kevin Grover. He didn't look much older than Carl. He was of average height, medium brown complexion with dark brown eyes. Kevin's hair was neatly kept in a small black-brown tapered cut close to his head. His physique looked as though he was a regular at the gym.

"This was your father at the age of twenty two. he had tried to run a fruit stand. He leased a corner building and managed a store for a brief while. He owed every grocer this side the Mississippi that loaned him equipment and stock," Grandma said smiling.

The children showed interest in hearing the back story of their dad. Grandma Alicia's smile turned evil.

"He managed to hook up with all these suppliers to set up all his pipe dreams," she said dryly.

"The fool sold everything and moved here from Youngstown. Said he held on to this picture to never lose sight of what he owed those people," she said.

Grandma Alicia humph'd ,tossing her head to the side before continuing. "He was a good looking boy and it didn't take long for all those fast tail girls around here to notice. He couldn't be discouraged by all the attention from the hussies. Your momma was the ring leader."

Carl's dreamy eyes bucked as he listened. Charles dark eyes darkened. Caroline's bright eyes were inquisitive. Grandpa's eyes were closed.

Grandma Alicia's hands flimsy in motion, waving back and forth as she spoke. "He worked for us and some of the neighbors cleaning out garages, running errands, cutting grass and odd jobs like that. He saved every nickel talking big 'bout how he owed some folks back home and wasn't gone stop 'til he had enough money to pay them."

Grandma Alicia didn't allow time for questions. "This here is a picture of your momma. Beautiful young lady, Caroline here looks just like her," she smiled at the memory. "She had started smelling herself. Ann graduated valedictorian of her high school class. Her head was pretty big at this time. She knew everything and nobody else knew anything," Grandma smirked.

"I caught Kevin looking at her the way a man looks at a woman. He never let her catch him. She got so mad that every other young man was sniffing around her but the one she wanted. She invented dirty little stories about him. She started a rumor that he was gay," she said.

The boys' mouths flew open, bottom lips threatening to reach their plates. They continued listening in silence. "Was he?" Caroline asked.

"What made her even madder is when he confronted her. She wanted him to be mad or admit it. He told her one day she would find out. Your momma being a lot like Caroline kept up so much mess. He lost a couple of his jobs at two of her best friend's homes," Grandma continued.

Grandpa Henry had a look of relief on his face. The whole story wasn't being told. Grandma Alicia continued on to the next picture.

Everyone was quiet. Nobody wanted to interrupt. Grandma Alicia pulled out the next picture. The third picture was of a baby. The picture could have been a boy or girl. It was a cute little chubby baby wearing a white christening gown.

"This is your mother's first born child that was put up for adoption," Grandma Alicia locked eyes with Carl. Caroline scratched her head. Charles and Grandpa didn't move. "She was sent away to relatives in North Carolina. I wasn't gone let her swelling body bring more shame to this family. She wasn't supposed to return."

Grandma shakes her head and continues on. "Being the bullheaded child that she was, she showed up six weeks after the baby should have been born telling us it died begging us to take her back. Your mother, Ann was swearing she was going to change her life, stop hanging out at night doing God knows what. Said she would attend church regularly. She did too, even joined the choir. Ann kept up so much mess she was the only person in the one hundred twenty year history asked to leave," Grandma said while laying the baby picture down and selecting the next.

"Fourth picture, your daddy bought his first little truck and this house," Grandma Alicia said with her index finger tapping the table proudly. "He asked for your mother's hand in marriage two years later. That gal was so surprised she said yes and then no." Grandma Alicia smiled.

"She told the boy they hadn't even had a date. She wasn't sure if he were the one. He took her to the picture show. She returned home walking on air." Her face softened. She looked to Henry.

"The next day, the day this picture was taken, Kevin marched right up to Henry and asked for your momma's hand in marriage. Henry took one look at Ann and said he would be honored." Grandma stopped talking looking to each of her grandchildren.

Fighting back the overwhelming feeling to cry, Carl began to sweat.

Grandpa Henry emphatically shook his head side to side. The dining room floor vibrated when he landed on his knees. He prayed for the children, forgiveness and evil to be removed. Grandma talked louder.

"Oh let me finish telling you about the baby," Grandma Alicia said, lowering the wedding picture and picking up the third photo. "This baby lives up the street from us now. He's eighteen years old and a senior at the high school you two attend. He was removed from his first adoptive parents. The state of Ohio placed him in Sister Hattie Mays' care from church. You all know Sister Mays."

Sweat was drenching Carl from head to toe. Caroline was intrigued. Charles was indifferent. Grandpa silently talked with God.

Grandma Alicia was pointing at Caroline. "You know your brother quite well don't you? Sister Hattie renamed him Brandon after that no good brother of hers."

The silence was finally broken. All questions were directed to Caroline.

Carl was waving his hands in the air, shaking his head. His heart racing, chest muscles tightened, sweat dripping down into his food. "You knew this was our brother and you didn't tell us! What kind of cold hearted person are you? You would keep something like that from me and Charles," he screamed.

Caroline grinned. "I don't keep anything from Charles."

Carl became quiet. His chest was heaving up and down with every breath. He wanted to beg Grandma Alicia to put the lid back on Pandora's Box. Instead through seething eyes, he stayed quiet and listened intently as the next picture was being revealed.

"In this picture your parents had been married a year. They were celebrating their anniversary along with the arrival of their first born son. Carl Kevin Grover."

Alicia's manner of speaking showed disappointment and disgust as she continued. "You were a sickly little thing born three months early. The doctors say you were a miracle, said most babies born that early have a low birth rate. Not you," she said sounding sarcastic. "You weighed in at seven pounds, seven ounces. Everybody said had your momma went full term you would have been a ten pound baby."

Charles interrupted. "Grandma they look so sad in this picture. Shouldn't they be smiling if they were celebrating?"

Grandma paused and looked at Grandpa. His head slowly turning side to side he responded.

"You done started it now, ain't no sense in trying to back out or sugar coat it. Just remember this got nothing to do with God. You did this and that is to come of it." Grandpa Henry left the table.

What came next changed Carl's life forever. Astounding, devastating news was to be revealed. As it was told Grandma didn't flinch.

"We never did meet your daddy."

"Wait a minute. What do you mean you never met my dad? My dad is Kevin Grover. I was named after him. My name is Carl Kevin Grover. I've been told all my life, we look just a like. Please Grandma Alicia tell me Kevin Grover is my dad?" Carl spoke barely above a whisper, his usually confident baritone voice quivering. He couldn't contain the tears building in his eyes.

Grandma Alicia continued. "Your momma was pregnant when she accepted that boy's marriage proposal and full well knew it! Again we couldn't get her to admit who the daddy was if she even knew," Grandma stated.

That fifth picture Carl stole out the hat box and carried in his wallet.

As Grandma Alicia continued, Carl spoke to himself. He was loud enough for all to hear. "Who was this woman that I called mom? She had me fooled into thinking she was a saint. Who is my biological father?, why do I look so much like someone who I do not share blood?"

Grandma Alicia was quiet now. Peacefully she sipped her jar of water, staring at the tormented look on her grandson's face. She smiled.

It appeared Caroline's heart was truly aching. She spoke between uncontrollable sobs and gasps.

"Grandma, if Kevin was not my dad, I do not want to know." Her alto voice had turned soprano. "You have no heart, how could you crush my brother! I am not the evil one. May I please be excused?" Caroline asked.

Grandma Alicia did not speak. She wore the eerie smile that Caroline had replaced with tears.

Grandpa Henry returned to the dining room. He looked at each child. He raised his hands above his head, dropped to his knees. The house shook as he landed.

Grandma left the table. She went into the kitchen as Grandpa was praying for forgiveness. She came back to the table, the mason jar full of ice water. It was a sign there was plenty more to be told.

Without asking, Carl got up to exit the dining room. Grandma Alicia was on his heels within seconds.

"Boy, if you don't sit your disrespectful behind back in that chair. As I have stated time and time again, I will not be overrun in my own home!"

Carl's eyes reddened. He was raised to believe in God. He was brought up to honor thy mother and father, respect your elders. In that instance he could stomach no more of this self righteous old woman.

His long arms revealed balled fists at his sides. Heaving in air, an intense expression on his face, he continued walking. He reached the front door. Carl turned and faced Grandma Alicia. "I don't want to hear another word from you. How do I know you are not making this up? Get it right old lady, this is my mother's house bought by her husband. So you don't get to tell me or my siblings what we cannot do in our home!" Carl stormed out the front door.

Caroline followed fifteen minutes later. The grin was back on her face. She had unleashed a tirade to be remembered on Grandma Alicia before making her exit.

Carl and Caroline waited for a half hour. Charles never showed. They sat in silence. Caroline reached for Carl in the darkness. She led him to the house.

Upon entering the house they were greeted by Charles. He had a faint smile on his lips. His eyes weren't smiling. Carl and Caroline brushed by him.

Charles took a seat at his usual place at the table. Before doing so, he pulled out chairs for his siblings. All heads bowed, they accepted his invitation to finish the madness.

It was now two o'clock in the morning. School was not an option this Monday morning. The entire family had been up all night.

Grandma Alicia pulled out the sixth picture as if the
conversation had never been interrupted. "This here is a
picture of the three of you going to church with me after
God spoke to me. I forgave my child again." She
explained the photo to Carl. "There were some conditions.
She was to tell Kevin that you were not his child and reveal
who your daddy was. I told her I didn't need to know but it
was just a dreadful sin that she would let Kevin keep
slaving to provide for a child that wasn't his. I knew in my
heart of hearts your Daddy knew you were no kin to him
but he loved you anyway despite being taken by that
Jezebel you called momma."

Carl held on to both sides of his chair. He locked
eyes with his Grandmother. Everything went blank. He
couldn't hear. He couldn't see. He couldn't speak.

Chapter 21

A Fractured Mind

There were tubes all over this chubby kid in the bed adjacent to his. There were pictures of cartoon characters all over the walls painted way too brightly. And that smell.

Charles began regaining focus. A man had visited. He looked like Grandpa Henry might have twenty years ago. He was wearing a Rainbow Babies and Children smock.

It was early morning when the strange man nudged him. As he regained consciousness he saw the man was sitting by his bed.

The man seemed familiar to Carl. He looked a lot like Grandpa Henry although much younger. Maybe this was one of his Uncles they had lost touch with so many years ago.

"Hello," Carl said clearing his throat.

"Hello, there young man, how are you feeling?" The stranger responded. "I was at church and heard that one of Sister Mays' young'uns was brought in. I work here you know so I thought I'd stop by and see how you doing from time to time if that's okay with you," the stranger asked.

Carl didn't get a chance to respond. The doctor came in followed by his grandparents and siblings, all of them.

The strange man from church nodded to Grandpa Henry. He acknowledged Grandma Alicia with a knowing smile. The stranger made eye contact with Brandon James. He left with his held bowed.

Carl greeted them all as they filed into the room pulling the curtain behind them. Everyone had a somber look on their face.

Carl tried to sound chipper. "Hey, what's everybody so sad about. I'm gone be fine right, Doc? I just didn't get enough to eat today and passed out or something. Hey Doc, can you please tell me what happened?"

The doctor extended his right hand for Carl to shake. As he reached for the side of the hospital bed to raise him self, he noticed tubes everywhere. There was an IV in the back of his hand, there had been a catheter implanted in his private parts. There were machines beating to there own rhythm slightly placed behind his bed. The machine in the corner looked like the EKG machine shown on all the TV shows. "Oh my God it is bad!" Carl screamed.

The doctor told him to take it easy. He said he would explain but he needed him to calm down.

Caroline was crying, Grandma and Grandpa were praying. Charles was staring in disbelief. Brandon was staring the hardest He looked at his hands, then at Carl's.

Finally the doctor began to speak. "I am Doctor Kale. I will explain your situation after I ask a few questions. "What is your name, do you know where you are, and do you know any of the people in the room? One more question, what day of the week is it?"

Carl answered all questions elaborating on the last. "Today is Monday, we didn't have dinner because Grandma Alicia opened Pandora's Box. The whole family was up late so we didn't go to school. She was giving us a family lesson about my Jezebel momma, not knowing who my dad is and informing me of an older brother who is standing right there and .."

Dr. Kale interrupted. "Son you have been in the hospital for about a week and a half. Today is Thursday. You were brought in by ambulance Monday morning around six o'clock almost two weeks ago."

The doctor was reading from the medical chart at the foot of the bed. "When we were done working on you, you would not speak. It appeared you could not hear anyone. You were in a catatonic state. We are feeding you intravenously and monitoring your vitals."

He explained the purpose of each tube inserted into Carl violating his space. "We are unable to diagnose what might have caused your condition. From what we have monitored thus far, you should recover physically. You will need to watch what you eat. Never pick up the unhealthy habit of tobacco. You may have just been stressed or clinically depressed is what has been determined for your mental health. We have never seen such a case in some one so young. I will be sending in a counselor to talk with you from our Peers to Peers Group. Would you prefer speaking with a male or female counselor within your age group," the doctor asked.

"Doc, I don't know what you mean catatonic. I've been healthy all my life. I feel great. There is nothing wrong with me. I need to get back home to finish a very important conversation with Grandma Alicia." Carl responded.

"Son, you will be going home soon. I cannot within good conscious let you leave without speaking to a professional. They may be better equipped to diagnose why this happened to you. I want to prevent it from happening again. You understand don't you?" Dr. Kale asked.

Carl frowned at the Doctor and his family.   All of them were gawking at him. He decided to go along with it. He was anxious to see what the seventh picture held.

Brandon volunteered to be there for Carl if needed. Carl boisterously stated that wouldn't be necessary.

He spoke with the psychiatric nurse on staff after refusing to speak with a peer.

Satisfied with all of his answers, she suggested that he be released and there was no need for counseling unless he felt the need to talk.

That Friday he was released. The grandparents came to pick him up and never mentioned the 'incident' as it came to be known. They continued on with the pictures that night.

Chapter 22

Reminiscent

Everyone took their usual seats around the table.

Grandma Alicia repeated her ritual, big glass of ice water,

superior attitude. Grandpa continued his ritual as well,

prayer, lots and lots of prayer.

The unmentioned consensus of the children was

Grandpa should have stopped this day one. Family secrets

should remain family secrets.

"I think picture number seven will make sense to

you, now that you know what type of momma you had."

Grandma Alicia passed the picture around the table. She started with Charles. He looked bewildered. Charles attempted to pass it to Caroline who looked as though she wanted to snatch it out of his hand.

Grandma interrupted. "No, your Grandfather get's to see it next." Grandpa refused to look at it and passed it on to Caroline. She stared at the picture, then at Carl.

"You show that picture to your brother and you show it to him now. This has gone on far too long," Grandma demanded. "I can't have this on my record when I meet my Maker. I should have dealt with that demon seed child long before the Devil took her lying, conniving behind from us."

Caroline was frantically shaking her head. "If my mother was all the things you say she was you passed them down to her." Screaming loudly she continued. "God will not accept you into his kingdom. Only the Good will ever meet God. Any one as cruel as you will never see eternal life. Your fate will be eternal damnation. The right to burn in hell just as you deserve!"

Caroline's long hair was loosely flying around. She was making hand gestures pointing to herself and Grandma Alicia. "I will meet you in Hell because I will never, ever be able to forgive you for this. I will welcome Hell just to make sure your eternal Hell never ends!" Caroline and Alicia had a stare down. Caroline began slowly ripping the picture in half.

Grandma Alicia moved quickly. Before Caroline could tear the photo again, Grandma had wrestled it from Caroline's hands. She went into her room and came back with the picture taped.

Carl sat there for a moment in a state of vertigo. "What could be making you all so crazy about this picture? I have to see it," he said.

Grandma locked eyes with Carl. "Do not pass out again. Be a man. Take this picture and study it long and hard. Don't be a coward like the excuse of a man that sits at this table." She said with a determined look in Grandpa's direction.

Grandpa drops to his knees and prays aloud.

God remove this devil from my presence, he continues praying silently. When he is done, tears are streaming down his face. His nose is running. His eyes are different. His eyes. He stands to his feet. His nostrils flared, his balding head glistening with sweat, eyebrows arched, he heads towards Grandma Alicia.

The children are frightened. They've never seen Grandpa angry. The walk to the eight seat dining room table seems to have taken him eight minutes to stand defiant in front of Grandma. His huge frame shadowing Alicia's petite body.

For the first time since she started this disentangling of the family, she is visibly shaken. Carl stood up. He didn't realize he was standing.

Grandpa kneels in front of Grandma, she seems to relax. He is quickly on his feet. His Barry White voice deeper.

"I have had just about enough. These children are all I have. You are trying to snub your nose at God's gifts! As evil as are only child may have been, we were not up for God's challenge. We felled Him and our daughter miserably. Now instead of dropping to your knees and repenting in Jesus' name you are spreading more of the devil's madness!"

The roaring of his voice had them all scared. "Wake up woman. Know this, I am no weak man, I am a God-fearing man who has made a terrible mistake. I married an evil woman. Now you want to make the spawn of my child as bitter? Children, get in the car now,"

Grandpa bellowed.

Caroline and Charles were frozen in their seats.

Carl was standing but unable to move. Grandma was

holding that seventh picture close to her heart.

Grandpa continued to speak. "For the love of

Christ, every child at this table, get up. Get your behinds

one clean outfit and get in the car. If you stay here you will

be destroyed.," he pleaded.

Grandpa tried reasoning with the children. He

tried to convince them to leave. "My God son, you

suffered a massive heart attack at seventeen years of age.

You Caroline are pregnant at fifteen. Charles, I see the

same evilness in the woman who was supposed to nurture

you. It's not right. I can't stay here. God has spoken

through me. I'm given a reprieve to do right. Let's just

walk away. I cannot in good conscious walk out on you.

I'm begging you to come with me. I'll be in the car,"

Grandpa said.

Grandma Alicia rose to her feet. She growled.

"Where do you get off trying to take my children? I don't

care if you go, you were never here anyways. You will not

take my babies!"

Grandpa spun around in the front door. "Woman,

don't you say another word. These were Ann's babies. No

matter what madness you try to place in their heads. They

know she loved them unlike you who are incapable of

love," he shouted. "God knows I tried. I hung in there

with your mess for forty one years. I have had it. You

keep the house and everything in it," he said.

Grandpa had his hand on the brass door knob. He

turned it left then right. He stopped. Standing tall, he

connected eye to eye with Grandma Alicia. "You are no

saint yourself but I will not humiliate you in front of these

kids. I will not tell your dirty little secrets. What I will do, is get as far away from you as possible before you cost me the ultimate price of freedom. Go on, this is the part where you call me names, cuss me from A to Z. Tell me how much of a weakling I am. Sunday you'll stand up in front of the whole congregation." He smirked, shaking his head. "You'll testify telling everyone just how lucky you are that God blessed you with me and these children. Don't you know God sees it all and the worst fate is dealt a false prophet?"

A noticeable calmness came over Grandpa Henry. He opened the front door. He turned around with a smile. "I am going up the road to pick up Brandon, your oldest sibling. When we get back, I expect you all to be in the yard. I cannot step foot in this house of evil again."

Grandpa swung open the door so hard it shook threatening to loose from the hinges.

Chapter 23

Walk Away

The children surrounded the car waiting on Grandpa
to unlock the doors. They peered into the windows.
Charles tried the doors several times. Nothing seemed to
move Grandpa. The three of them stood outside by the car.
No one talked. All eyes were on the ground.

The locks popped. Startled, Caroline and Carl both
reached for the front door on the passenger side. Carl
relented and got in the backseat. Charles was already
seated behind Grandpa.

Grandpa got out of the car with his head hanging down, shoulders slumped forward. He walked toward the house. He held the door open. The children followed suit in a single file line. Gloom and doom awaiting them on the other side of that door.

Charles walked in without hesitation.

Caroline paused and turned to Carl. "If you don't want to do this, I will leave with you," she said. "It's your call."

Carl's knees buckled. He couldn't find the strength to keep walking. Caroline and Grandpa rushed to his aid. "Just let me sit down a minute. I know I can handle this. I have to be able to look the old geezer in the eye. Just let me get my bearings. I will be alright," he said.

His comments fell on deaf ears. Grandpa and Caroline looked as though he was going to have a relapse.

Carl did something he hadn't done unless in church on Sunday in a very long time. Silently he prayed. He got up with a new found strength.

He grabbed Grandpa's hand and held it. "You are not a weak man, if I live to be your age, I would consider myself a King. I would be blessed to turn out like you."

Carl did the same with Caroline, "You are not evil. You have a big heart and a wild imagination," they both chuckled. "I love you for who you are not what everybody perceives you to be," he said.

Carl looked for Charles. Alliances had been formed. Grandpa, Caroline and Carl were doing battle with Grandma Alicia and Charles.

Chapter 24

Hurricane Alicia Brooks

Grandma never left the table. She was clutching the seventh picture to her heart. Her mason jar of ice water was half empty. Charles was sitting by her side.

In true form, Grandma Alicia began speaking as if the fight witnessed hours ago had never occurred. "This picture here is of Carl and Charles' father. That jezebel of a momma of yours cheated on Mr. Grover twice. Your momma liked weak men like her Daddy here," she said pointing nonchalantly to Grandpa Henry. "He kept forgiving and forgiving over and over until you were born Charles."

Charles said nothing. He looked straight ahead. His focus was intense.

"That's what broke his spirit. He knew there was no way you could have been his. He suffered a hernia and was told he could father no more children shortly after his one child he bore with your momma. Caroline is the only child that Kevin and Ann had together. You other two are her dirty little secrets, bastards actually," she said.

Caroline breathed a sigh of relief. "So Grandma is the money mine, is that what this is leading up to, there is some sort of clause to reveal who their real father is upon my parent's death," she asked.

"Unbelievable, you are truly ill in the head. After all I have tried to do for you! After the talk we've had not five minutes ago! All you can think about is money. Would you really let Charles and I fend for ourselves,

Caroline…how do we know any of what she is saying is true!" Carl stared at his sister. "Already you are turning on us, what the hell," he screamed. Grandpa was standing behind him as if he was a fragile piece of China about to crumble to the floor.

Carl was not about to let that happen. He refused to give them the satisfaction of watching him crumble up and die.

Carl snatched the picture out of Grandma's hand. He stared long and hard. He looked for some sort of resemblance. The man in the picture had a stocky build. He and Ann were about the same height. He could have been Brandon's dad. He and Charles were short for men. Both were of stocky builds. Carl is six feet even with a slim muscular build.

Carl returned to his seat. He took a deep breath. "What's his name?"

Grandma looked confused. She didn't answer right away. She gulped down what was left of her water, paused and turned to Caroline. "You my dear are a lovely child. I hope one day you will find it in your heart to forgive me. I thought it was time to get everything out in the open. No the money isn't all yours. Kevin being the weakling that he was let that no good liar daughter of mine trick him into believing your brothers were his up until the day they were leaving for New York," Grandma said.

Carl and Caroline had been asking for years what had happened in New York. Their ears became radars. It was finally about to be revealed. Carl couldn't stop himself from interrupting.

"Grandma, what is the gentlemen's name in the picture, I would really like to know. Does he live around here, Does he know he has two handsome young sons, did you know anything about this Grandpa," Carl asked.

Grandpa didn't respond. Grandma stood up swiftly. "I am tired. We will finish this tomorrow. Goodnight Miss Grover. Goodnight to the young Misters Smith." She strutted away from the table with her head held high like a peacock.

Before she reached the hallway leading to the stairs, Charles pounced like a wild ally cat. "Hold the hell up, old lady. This was never in the plan. You told me that my dad was this Kevin Grover person," he said. "You are lying, he is probably both our dads. I told your crazy old ass, I don't trust the living and walk careful around the dead. Did you think I was excluding you?"

Charles was in her face. Spit flying out of his mouth. His hands balled into fists. "I don't think you want to walk away from this right now. You may want to double check your facts. Sit down before I sit you down!"

Not a tear fell down Charles' cheek. His eyes turned bloodshot red. He seemed to have grown five inches overnight and there had been a rage never seen nor heard exuding from him.

Caroline and Carl sat and stared at their little brother. Grandpa's lack of reaction was even more frightening. He did not pray, he did not speak, he did not move. The tension inside was threatening to blow the roof sky high.

Grandma Alicia stood frozen in time. Charles was in a demonic trance with a killer grip on her wrists. Their arms trembling, suspended in mid air. Grandma's trembling caused by fear. Charles', pure uninhibited hate, and the desire to do bodily harm.

Finally Grandpa stood in place at the table. He walked toward Charles slowly. He got down on bended knee. He was eye level with Charles. Grandpa placed a hand on each of Charles' shoulders. He waited until Charles' grip on Grandma was subsiding. He quickly stood, picked Charles up and slammed him on the center of the table.

"Boy I heard more than I care to hear about the goings on of you and your Grandmother. Your Momma knew you would all go crazy. She voided all that mess you been reading. The last will and testament is locked in the vault at the bank. Only the Manager and I have a key. This madness is going to end tonight," Grandpa said.

"Alicia sit your behind down and tell this boy who his father is! Charles I think the real demon lives inside of you. Take your butt to my seat and think about your actions. What were you going to do, kill your own grandmother! None of you kids asked for this. It's the hand you were dealt," Grandpa Henry yelled.

He continued shouting, "What in God's name is wrong with you?" Caroline, you are unusually quiet so I can just about figure you know more than you're letting on. Carl, you are a good man, you deserve better. God got good things planned for you. Charles, I will continue to pray for your soul, I will rebuke the devil in the name of the Lord."

Caroline and Carl hadn't moved. Charles was seated at the end of the table. Grandma was at the other end.

Charles had finally done what no one had accomplished in nine years. Tears flowed steadily down Grandma's face. She didn't bother to wipe the tears away.

The tables had turned and Grandpa had the upper hand. He began to finish the story. "I am going to go around this table with pure facts. I will start from the oldest and work my way down to the youngest. I will not be interrupted. If you have questions you will wait until I have told your whole story."

Grandpa exited the dining room. He was absent from the table a half hour. Everyone waited. No one spoke. No one made eye contact.

He returned with a serving tray filled with a pitcher of ice tea, lemon slices, and bucket of ice, sugar cubes, butter cookies and two stacks of napkins.

"Okay Alicia, I guess I got to clean up your mess again." Grandpa started to speak matter-of-fact while walking around the table placing drinking glasses in front of everyone. His movements were methodical. His speech clear and deliberate. "You wanted these kids to know what kind of woman Ann was so that they could see you in a different light. You were no saint. Ann was not my biological child but you better believe she was my daughter. I loved that child as if she were my own. I would have done anything for her," he confessed.

Grandma looked as though she wanted to say something. Grandpa's long arm came up so fast. The palm of his hand halting Grandma. Obediently she lowered her head.

Grandma looked beaten. Henry had revealed her secret. She was no better than the daughter she criticized.

Grandpa went on. "I am not going to give these children all the dirty little details but I think you should not judge anyone. You and I know what we've been through. I told you years ago I turn it over to God and he's working it out. Alicia, I sat back these past years and let you tear this family to shreds. I talked to God about it, if I hadn't it would have eaten me alive," Grandpa said.

He stirred the ice tea with the wooden spoon. He began speaking again. "We don't go no where, we have no friends. I can't remember the last time anyone visited after the kids died. The only outing we have is to church functions. I'm invited only when you are not around. You have been so mean and hateful." He sighed before continuing. "After forty one years I have thought about throwing in the towel. This crap you been pulling on these kids the last two weeks have just about pushed me over the edge. I cannot and will not tolerate it a moment longer. It stops tonight!" Grandpa said.

He exhaled before speaking. "Son, Carl it's your call do you really need to know who your biological father is. Wouldn't you rather go on with the memories of the great man who raised you?" Don't answer me now. I want to give you a few minutes to think about it."

Before Carl could speak, Grandpa was making the rounds at the table. He dropped five ice cubes in each glass.

As soon as Grandpa returned to his seat Carl turned to face him. "Not only do I want to know Grandpa, I need to know. Please tell me who James Brandon Smith is as a person."

Grandma pulled her chair in closer to the table. Her face brightened with the anticipation of what was to be said.

"You should not perk up because of someone's misery. You are not going to come out shining in this little piece of family history," Grandpa said.

Grandma's smirk was replaced with a scowl directed at Carl. It was confirmation for him. She never liked him now he was going to find out why.

"Smith is Sister Mays' brother, the young man who visited you in the hospital."

Carl's dark brown skin went gray. He said nothing, he continued listening.

"He had taken an abnormal liking to the girls before he met God. He preferred them young. When they are so insecure and trying to find their way. As beautiful a girl your momma was she felt ugly inside. Your Grandmother made a religion of telling her daily how unattractive she was. That girl went out with any man that asked. There is no telling what type of crap she put up with or things she did just trying to feel something, anything but ugliness.

The 'saint' at the head of the table saw to making that child hate herself. She became so withdrawn. She stopped hanging out with her friends, wouldn't talk to nobody. I sat her down one day and explained as best I could men and women are different. A girl who only has boy friends is gone find herself labeled something she didn't want to be called," he said.

Grandpa took a long pause. He passed a disgusted look to his wife. "Low and behold it happened, right here in her home by her own mother. Smith new that child was insecure and unhappy. He took advantage of her in the worst possible way."

Grandpa got up. He went around the table with the pitcher of ice tea and started pouring. He said aloud, "I got to finish this."

He returned to the seat next to Carl. He stared at him. He reached for his hand. He quickly released it. He stood again this time picking up the bowl of lemons placing two slices in each glass.

Grandpa returned to his seat with a tormented expression. "Okay Carl, I'm just gone come right out and say it. Smith is your grandfather and father."

Grandma let out an incredulous sigh and drops her head.

Carl finds his voice. "I don't understand. How could he be my father and grandfather?" He would have to ...my mother and... her!" He said pointing at his grandmother.

Carl stared at Grandma Alicia. His throat became dry. He reached for the tea. The taste was just as bitter as the news delivered.

Alicia couldn't lift her head. She refused to show her face.

Grandpa immediately got up grabbing the sugar cubes. He placed four cubes in each glass and walked out on the front porch leaving everyone in complete silence.

Carl sat there staring at the crown of Grandma's head, daring her to show her face.

Grandma reared her ugly head. She was talking so fast. Her teeth were clinched, her fist hitting the table with every syllable. "Your daddy and the man I should have married fathered your no good momma and you! She knew JB loved me. With her looking as I did twenty years earlier of course he had mistaken her for me that one night. That little jezebel had him liquored up and she raped him. He did not rape her. She went airing this mess to the Reverend Cole. That's why God took her away from here! JB was the man I was supposed to marry. The devil was stewing in that child. She couldn't let that happen. She got pregnant with you just to add salt to an open wound!"

Glasses and plates shook. The blows to the table became harder. "I told her she was ugly inside out. I told her she wasn't gone amount to nothing. I told her she was the seventh child, as evil and low down as a rattle snake. I prayed for her death!"

Grandma abruptly stood. She headed for the porch. Fury showing in her eyes, revenge in her heart. Grandpa was not to escape the wrath of Hurricane Alicia Brooks.

Chapter 25

Broken Spirits

The French doors open very slowly. His legs were like tree trunks in a storm. They were struggling to stay planted being pulled from their comfort zone by heavy winds. "We are going to end this right here tonight," Grandpa Henry said as he dragged himself in the house. "You children get washed for bed. I will see you in the morning. God bless the child..." he said barely above a whisper.

Alicia was standing in Grandpa's path. He did not acknowledge her presence. He repeated the nightly ritual. Grandpa walked toward Alicia as if she was transparent.

Alicia stood there mouth hanging open. Right at the moment where they could have collided, Alicia stepped to the side. Grandpa continued walking.

Charles, Caroline and Carl all pushed their chairs back from the table and started toward their bedrooms. Carl stopped. He looked back as did Caroline. Their eyes met.

He never turned to face the children. "You can run but you won't get far. You will one day want to know the end. This thing will gnaw at you until it consumes you." Grandpa said.

"Grandpa, we aren't really doing anything at school these last two weeks. We all got excellent grades. I'll be graduating. Please can we sit down and get this over with," Carl asked.

Grandma takes her seat at the head of the table. Charles sits beside her. Grandpa, Caroline and Carl are standing in a circle. He looks from Carl to Caroline, "okay."

Grandpa waited for all to be seated. He went back to the serving tray. He passed out six cookies to all of them talking while continuing his display. "Nobody has eaten anything today. Tonight we are having cookies and tea for dinner."

No, no, no!" Grandma starts hollering. "You can't do this Henry. You can choose when you have had enough. You can walk away. Let's stop this now," she exclaims.

Grandpa smiled a sad smile. "Life is so funny. A barrel of laughs. Twisted little jokes hurtful things to innocent people. Didn't have to be like this if we adhered to God's laws. It's all over. It's time. I told you not to blame this on God. You did this, " he said.

For the first time in hours Caroline spoke. "Okay Grandpa I don't want to finish. I'm scared. I have lied. You never touched me. Grandma you've been great to me. Carl, I couldn't ask for a better big brother. Charles I love you. Let's just go back to the beginning. Let's start all over. Please," she begged.

"I am pregnant. I am just like my mother. I will tell you that it is not Grandpa's child and it is definitely not Brandon's. I knew I felt a closeness to him. I had no idea he was my brother. Let's just stop now," Caroline continued.

Charles walked swiftly to Caroline. She unexpectedly pushed him away. Caroline laid her head on Carl's shoulder and wept uncontrollably. He put his arms around her. He told her everything was going to be okay. Rather he believed it wasn't important.

Caroline turned to Charles." Tell them," she said.

Charles smiled at Caroline, then at Carl. He took his seat

back at Grandma's side.

Part II -*Severed Family Ties*- Coming soon

Website: www.pcpcmarks.com

Reviews: www.freewebs.com/pcmarks

Contact: pcpcmarks@aol.com

ISBN: 978-0-6151-6093-1

Library of Congress Control Number: 2007906929